For B|+
granddaughter , with all my
love,
                Pa

AMERICAN JOURNEYS:

Stories of Three Lives

Erwin Hargrove

iUniverse, Inc.
Bloomington

iUniverse books may be ordered through booksellers or by contacting:

iUniverse
1663 Liberty Drive
Bloomington, IN 47403
www.iuniverse.com
1-800-Authors (1-800-288-4677)

Because of the dynamic nature of the Internet, any Web addresses or links contained in this book may have changed since publication and may no longer be valid. The views expressed in this work are solely those of the author and do not necessarily reflect the views of the publisher, and the publisher hereby disclaims any responsibility for them.

Any people depicted in stock imagery provided by Thinkstock are models, and such images are being used for illustrative purposes only.

Certain stock imagery © Thinkstock.

ISBN: 978-1-4502-6376-4 (sc)
ISBN: 978-1-4502-6375-7 (ebook)

Printed in the United States of America

iUniverse rev. date: 1/11/2011

To Julie

PREFACE

This is the story about the lives of three men from 1930 to 2000. They leave North Carolina and become a psychiatrist, a historian, and a journalist. They work, respectively, at Cornell Medical School, Brown University, the University of Virginia, and the *Baltimore Sun*. The five wives tell their stories in a chapter devoted to them. John tries to combine psychotherapy with medical psychiatry against professional opposition. George is a strong scholar who values academic achievement but resists political correctness and political intolerance in universities. Clay loves the life of newspapers but opposes the movement toward newspapers as a business. Each finds his own path in these labyrinths. Each of them is combating long-term trends in modern life that favor technology, specialization, and organizational imperatives.

This novel is a labor of love, because I have been able to present my understanding of work, marriage, and life, not through exposition but through the lives of the people I have created. A few stories from my life are seen in their lives, but each character is himself and not me. The four of us lived through the same periods of history, so perhaps this is also a portrait of a generation.

CHAPTER 1

Early Days
North Carolina, 1930–1948

It was not a small town, yet one would not call it a city. It was a paradise for boys and girls. They could ride their bikes along wide streets under spreading trees. The houses with broad front lawns were set back from the streets. Everything seemed in proportion to everything else. Of course, that was true only for the small number of better-off white families. The blacks, then called Negroes or colored, were on the bottom, with a larger class of white workers, manual and salaried, sandwiched in between. Things were not so good for them, especially in the Depression years of the thirties, but small boys of "good families," born in 1930, had no feeling for such things.

The three boys—John McDonald, George Logan, and Clay Page— knew they were privileged, because they lived in big houses and because their fathers seemed to be prominent in town, but they had little feeling for the lives of the less privileged. Their parents were friends, and the other boys and girls they knew had parents just like their parents. They went to an elementary school with children like themselves. Many teachers in their schools, including high school, had taught their parents. It just seemed natural. There were a few high schools, including one for black students, and a variety of students attended the high school with these boys. Relations among the students were very democratic, but there was little contact with other students in the city except in sports.

John was black-headed and angular, and he was a leader in everything. He caught passes in football, was president of the high school student council, and was popular with the girls. George was quiet and thoughtful, a good student. He had sandy hair and gray eyes, and he spent a lot of time by himself, reading everything from comic books to Dickens. Clay was short and blond and extremely amiable. He could charm a bird out of a tree. The boys were inseparable. It was not clear to many why they were so close.They had plenty of other friends; it was just a fact. Clay was the glue,

1

because he was so steady. The other two needed a friend like Clay. John was not comfortable in his family because of his stepmother, so friends were very important to him. George was a bookworm who often needed to be pulled out of himself.

They went to the same kindergarten. Miss Raffington was, as they used to say, a "maiden lady" who picked up the children each day in a large touring car and delivered them home the same way. She was a familiar sight, driving slowly around town with a car packed with little people. The children could not tell you what they had done at kindergarten. The ride was the exciting part.

The boys went to the same grade school and had "old maid" teachers, some of whom were nice and some of whom were mean. Miss Ozenberger, the fourth-grade teacher, styled her hair in long ringlets, and she was rumored to wear bloomers. She locked misbehaving boys in the nurse's room. One miscreant once wiggled out of the window and ran home. After that, she took his corduroy knickers and hung them up in the class cloakroom. The students howled with laughter every time she did it.

John remembered the day that school let out in late May after his second-grade year. He could feel rain in the air. The clouds were tumbling, and the wind was rising in his face. As he ran home, he had the wonderful thought that he was free for three months to do exactly what he wanted. It was a great feeling of release, and he never forgot it.

None of them knew any "colored" people well except maids and waiters at the country club. George remembered an old man named Jack who worked in the yard and garden for his grandfather. Jack wore a woman's silk stocking on his head as a cap. The old man and young George would sit in the backyard and visit, and sometimes George's grandmother would join them. She was extremely fond of Jack. In later years, George remembered Jack's kindness and his soft laughter.

They all three thought of black people in this way. In later years, after they had left the South, they supported civil rights.

The three families went to the same Presbyterian church, which had been attended by their great-grandparents and likely their parents, too. The long sermons were accompanied by the swish of fans on hot days. They took Communion four times a year out of little shot glasses filled with grape juice. At least the Episcopalians down the street got wine. Presbyterians were Scots by descent, often called 'Scotch-Irish," because their forebears came from the Protestant, northern part of Ireland, while the Episcopalians were mostly English in background.

The preacher they most remembered was Dr. Bob McIver, who had an honorary Doctor of Divinity. He wore a white suit and shoes in the summer and black clothes in the winter. He was against sin but didn't bring it up too much. His text was usually a legacy from the doctrine of predestination. God had plans for our lives, and we had to find out what they were and follow them. An implicit message for boys and men was this: they were to be "successful" in life. That did not necessarily mean they had to make a lot of money. One had to succeed in service to mankind, but in that time and place, success was given a worldly definition. One could not fail, and the fear of failure was ground into many young hearts. Their fathers certainly believed these things and preached them to the boys. They expected their sons to be like themselves, good men who were also successful.

John McDonald

John's mother, Dorothy, died in January 1939, just after he turned eight in October. She came home one Saturday afternoon after shopping. He was standing at the open front door and saw her as she slowly came up the walk. He would always remember the exhausted look on her face. Elsie Mae, the maid, cook, and lord of all things, became alarmed and called John's father, who was a doctor. He and Dr. Thompson, who had delivered John at one time, came to the house together. Dorothy had pneumonia and was taken to the hospital immediately. John lurked around her bedroom, but no one paid him much attention. He knew that his mother was really sick, and he felt very uncomfortable about it. His grandmother had told him that his mother had often been sick as a child. In fact, she used to faint in school, and all the other children hoped that Dorothy would faint so that they could go home while the teacher looked after her. Years later, when he read her letters, John found that she had had many unexplained illnesses.

Children were not allowed in hospitals in those days unless they were patients. On Wednesday night, he and his father sneaked up the fire escape to see his mother in her room. She opened her arms to John in a wonderful greeting, and he never forgot her shining face. His father later told him that she had been very worried about what would happen to John if she died. The report on Thursday was that she was getting better, but she was on her own, because neither penicillin nor sulfa existed then.

John went to school on Friday and came home for lunch as usual. He saw a number of family friends in the front hallway and living room when he opened the front door. His stomach told him something bad had happened, but no one spoke to him. Soon, his father appeared, led him upstairs to his bedroom, and told him that his mother had died. John cried a little and then said to his father, "Promise me that you will not marry again." Many years later, when he was training to be a psychiatrist, his psychoanalyst told him that he had been a "really smart boy." John had one parent left and wanted it to stay that way. His father promised but broke his promise within two years by marying, severing the bond that John had wanted to keep.

John wanted to go back to school that afternoon, as if nothing had happened, but the request was denied. Later on, he recalled that he moped around the house that weekend. He did not go to the funeral, because his grandmother thought that funerals were not for children, and for the rest of his life, he never knew on what day his mother had been buried. He had been denied the chance to grieve, but he did not learn this until many years later when he finally understood psychology better.

On a late summer afternoon in 1940 when John was in the backyard, he looked up to see his father and a young strawberry blonde woman approaching him. Both were wearing jodhpurs, because they had been riding. Young John had never seen the woman before. Once more, his stomach told him that something was wrong. John, Sr., introduced her as Kitty Reed. Young John held his breath and asked no questions.

In the fall, Kitty showed John her engagement ring. John, Sr., had told him nothing; the ring spoke for itself. They were married in December, and the newlyweds and young John moved to an apartment. They had to leave his grandmother's large, comfortable house on a double lot. Elsie Mae went with them and lived in a basement room. John asked through his father if he could call Kitty "mother." Her answer was no, and no reason was given.

Kitty set to work to reform John's table manners, telling him that his father had spoiled him. He had felt love, not spoiling, but affection for his father weakened as John, Sr., stayed in the background and let John and Kitty fight it out. John later figured out that she was jealous of him, and besides, she was trying to learn how to be married. He sometimes acted out, little of which he could remember, but his father would chase him around the bedroom on these occasions, slapping his bare legs with a belt.

Until then, John had been a good student, but his grades began to fall. He felt alone at home and thought of volunteering to live at the orphanage.

He also had dreams of running away from home. He needed his father, and when the doctor went out of town to see patients, John stayed awake at night, fearful that he would not come home.

George Logan

George's mother, Ophelia, was a Colonial Dame, a Daughter of the Confederacy, and one of the few young women in "society" who left Mobile. The inbreeding in that Old South city was marvelous, and a family was almost disgraced if one of its "girls" escaped town with a "foreign" husband. Ophelia was quite lovely, tall and willowy, with golden hair. She met Byrne Logan at Sweet Briar College when he came from the University of Virginia for a blind date. He swept her off her feet, and her parents could hardly reject a University of Virginia graduate who practiced law in a fourth-generation family firm. It took Ophelia some time to adjust to the more "democratic" mid-South of General Jackson rather than the South of Jefferson Davis. However, she eventually did adjust, because she wanted to be nice to everybody, even though she was a secret snob who valued old families and thought in terms of "good breeding," which really just meant old families. She also favored good-looking people over plain ones.

Byrne Logan was a litigator for banks and other local corporations whose work often took him to surrounding state capitals and sometimes the federal courts. George went to court when he could, to hear his father plead. He was fascinated with legal reasoning, which would leap over the uncertainties and reach for judgment. This may have explained his decision to become a historian. His mother perhaps contributed to his career choice as well, because she often told him stories about his forebears on both sides of the family. Her family had been planters and soldiers and, more recently, cotton brokers. They were Virginians who had come west and south and done well, first as planters and then as lawyers. His maternal grandmother, Gladys, and her brother, Charles, had traveled widely, living on and off in Paris and other European cities. Charles was an artist who sent many *objets d'art* home to grace family houses. There was nothing special about this except that it appealed to his mother and gave the family a little patina among other old families. George absorbed all this and later wrote a short history of his mother's family, which produced many interesting eccentrics and made for good stories.

Ophelia loved the theater and often acted in plays presented by the local Junior League. She sometimes arranged for George to play small boys in the plays, and he quickly developed a love of acting. He enjoyed being the center of attention, even though he was shy—or perhaps because of it. It was good training for a future college professor. Of course, he could have been a trial lawyer like his father, but he was captivated by history and used his dramatic skills in the classroom.

Clay Page

Catherine Page, Clay's mother, wrote poems and short stories, some of which were published in "little" magazines, and she also kept a diary that he read after her death. She came from Nashville and had studied English at Vanderbilt with Robert Penn Warren, John Crowe Ransom, and Alan Tate, the inventors of the new literary criticism that emphasized reading poetry for itself and the meanings conveyed rather than the biographies or histories of poets and poetry. She taught Clay her love of language.

Catherine was a private person with a few close women friends, who formed an informal book club for their intellectual life. She was also a "New Deal" Democrat but kept her views pretty much to herself. She attended the Presbyterian church but did not like it and gradually moved one block to Christ Episcopal Church. The prayer book English was so wonderful to her, and the liturgy held mysteries that she felt Presbyterians knew nothing about. Her banker husband attended both churches in order to keep his clients happy. He was the president of the biggest bank in town after all.

Alex Page followed in his father and grandfather's footsteps at the bank. He saw banking as a way of helping people rather than making money. A banker was in touch with people throughout the local economy, knew many of them well, and could help them as long as he had high banking standards. He loved his wife, and although he was not particularly literary, favoring mystery novels and American and English histories, he shared her politics, again quietly. His family had been typical southern Democrats, but his grandfather and father had admired Woodrow Wilson and FDR without being vocal about it. He read Catherine's written work and was a valuable touchstone as a general reader. Their happy marriage surely had an effect on Clay, who was happy by nature, confident, and trusting.

Boyhoods in Common

The three boys survived the dancing school, which their fathers had attended in their youth. They learned the fox-trot, and the girls learned all the dances. In high school, John was a star athlete. George was a scholar, and Clay was the newspaper editor. That was when they started to give serious attention to girls for the first time, but not to the girls they knew well from kindergarten, Sunday school, dancing school, and the country club. The perkiness and good looks of girls who were from other parts of town appealed to them. These girls didn't fit the country club mold and were less conventional about necking, drinking, and having a good time. But such girls would not commit to the three friends, because they knew the boys were going to places where they could not follow. These girls appeared at reunions in later years, looking pretty good.

High school was fun and not challenging. The three friends did well academically and had plenty of time left over for dating and drinking beer in joints on the highway, for the county was not a dry one. They went fishing and coon hunting with their fathers, often in the company of local men who knew where the fish were and had good coon dogs. These men were usually what they called "characters." They chewed tobacco and talked colloquial English as they ate catfish around the fire. In fact, despite their relatively sheltered childhoods, the boys developed an easy democratic style and respect for all kinds of people. Attending public schools, especially high school, had ensured this. They only segregated themselves in the summers when they played golf and tennis at the country club with boys of their own class.

The boys pretty much made up their own minds about where to apply for college. John set his sights on Yale, in part because his uncle, his father's brother, a lawyer in New York, had attended Yale. He scattered applications to Wesleyan, Williams, and Davidson, his insurance school; however, Yale was his goal, and he was eventually accepted. The Ivy League school was happy to have a southern boy in 1948. George's mother thought there was only one school, the University of Virginia; it was the icon of southern gentility to Ophelia. He was willing to go, but after a visit to Washington and Lee, he decided that he would get a better education in a smaller school. He and his father persuaded Ophelia that W. and L. was just as good as Virginia. After all, the boys wore jackets and neckties to class. Clay wanted to study journalism at the University of Missouri, because it had the best undergraduate school in the country. His parents wondered if he was shortchanging himself on a "liberal" education. He could have gone to UNC at Chapel Hill, but Clay was looking forward to future jobs and decided that Missouri would place him well.

All three families had comfortable summer houses on a lake in the western mountains, where the families vacationed each summer, and there, the boys talked endlessly about their futures. John, however, was especially apprehensive about Yale.

"I wonder what those eastern boys are like?" mused John. "Many of them are from eastern prep schools. What will they think of a country boy like me?" John was anything but a country boy, but this was the provincial way of talking. The answer to his question was beyond their experience.

"You have to show that you are smarter," said George. "You are taking a big leap, but that is your nature. You are not going to be confined by anything, including prep school boys."

George could have gone to Harvard or the University of Chicago; however, his parents' horizons were too short, and he was a self-starter who felt comfortable with his choice. He may have been the most "southern" of the three, perhaps because of his mother. Clay had newspaper work and writing in his blood, and he knew what he wanted to do. The other two were uncertain about their career choices. John was thinking of medicine, but George had no idea except that, while he admired his father and his work, he did not want to be a lawyer.

As they parted in September, they thought of the town as home. None of them expected to return home to work, but home was to be their secure base, not only for the college years, but for all of their lives as well. They left the town, but the town did not leave them.

CHAPTER 2

John
Yale and Medicine, 1948–1957

I had visited New York City to see Aunt Helen and Uncle Bob several times, but the visit on the way to New Haven was special. Their east-side apartment was to be a home away from home, and Manhattan was now a plate of oysters. We took a boat trip around the island, ate lobster in Sheepshead Bay, and saw *Gentlemen Prefer Blondes*, and I went to the Metropolitan Museum of Art. I was nervous driving up the Merritt Parkway to New Haven, not knowing a soul at Yale, but as soon as I walked into the old campus where the freshmen lived, I felt at home. This was to be my home for a year.

My roommate in Durfee Hall was Charlie Preston from Fort Worth, Texas. He had a big smile and laughed a lot, and sometimes he wore cowboy boots. No one was going to intimidate him. There were two very friendly boys across the hall, Bill and Joe from Massachusetts, who had gone to a minor New England prep school, so we banded together for the next four years.

Sixty percent of the freshman class had gone to prep schools, and seventy-five boys in the class had gone to Andover. A good number were from Lake Forest or Winnetka, suburbs outside Chicago or Shaker Heights in Cleveland, and comparable places. All of these boys were ahead of the game socially and academically for a time, because they had covered much of the freshman curriculum already.

Public school boys caught up and even surpassed the preppies academically, but few of them caught up socially. It was the difference between "white shoe" and "black shoe" boys. If one wore rep ties, tweed or cord jackets, and khaki pants and had a gray flannel suit, one was likely to be "shoe." Southern boys of a "good" background had an advantage here, because they had dressed that way at home. Loafers could substitute for white bucks only if one knew how to walk and a casual manner that scuffed their soles on the pavement.

9

Charlie and I eventually found plenty of friends, some from the South but not all. The four of us applied to Davenport College for sophomore year and lived in the same suite for three more years. The suite across the hall was occupied by friends from Baltimore, Memphis, New Orleans, and New Hampshire: Duff, Ronnie, another Joe, and John. I had several close friends, including Hugh, who was from Missouri. We became such fast friends that we had regular reunions of our own all our lives, even bringing our wives and children. Of course, we attended Yale reunions only to find that the social distinctions established at Yale still held.

I majored in English and took the requisite number of science courses for premed. And my grades were good. Charlie and I joined a fraternity, which provided a bar, a dining room, and more people to get to know. We were not within earshot of one of the six "senior societies," however. In our junior year, our class assembled in Branford College courtyard for Tap Day. Representatives of each of the societies descended from windows above and hit the shoulder of a desired recruit while they shouted the name of the society. Then the recruit was led off. It was an ignominious experience, separating the sheep from the goats. I was disillusioned to see faculty members doing some of the tapping.

The societies were the linchpin of Yale as a social institution. Freshmen who understood the system, usually from their schools, entered Yale with the ambition to get to the top, whether they wanted to ascend the ranks of the team sports, student publications, the political union, or Dwight Hall, the place for Protestants who believed in "Muscular Christianity." Skull and Bones took top athletes and big men on campus. Scroll and Key took the intellectually ambitious, as did Elihu. Wolf's Head took the editors of publications and so on. The societies met in secret, so one never knew what they did, but they were evidently sources of jobs and preferment throughout life. I remember a head of surgery at Cornell Medical School went to a Skull and Bones reunion every summer.

One of the best things about Yale was the visits to Manhattan, where friends and I often stayed with Aunt Helen and Uncle Bob. He loved to have Yale men around so that we could sing Cole Porter's football fight songs. They came up for football games, and we would go to fraternity parties afterward and sing the same songs. Uncle Bob was a smart man and a good lawyer, and he loved Yale with a passion, not just because of the songs. They were generous to us, taking us out to dinner and the theater on occasion.

Joe Stephens and I would slip off on the train to see plays in New York. One night, we saw Christopher Fry's *Sleep of Prisoners*, which was staged in St. James Episcopal Church on the east side. After the play, we went to Times Square and bought tickets to dance with the taxi dancers. I remember one hot number who was known as Angie, Queen of the Orpheum. She was practically in your pockets as you danced with her. One wondered how many Yale students had known her over the years. She was actually quite charming. When we ran out of money Joe tried to cash a travelers check but no one would cash it so we had to go back to New Haven. When I was in medical school in New York, I went to see if Angie was still there, and she was. I have often wondered what eventually happened to her.

Sheer silliness occupied much of our time. During our sophomore year, we had some dates from all-girl colleges and entertained them in our suite with what we called "beano," gin in a tub with a big block of ice. It was pretty lethal, and we drank much more than the girls did, which did not sit so well with them.

Despite such activities, we were learning and growing. The master of our college had a long-standing relationship with Robert Frost, and we sometimes gathered in the college common room to hear him speak his poetry. I remember feeling that Emerson and Thoreau were in the room. Only years later did I learn that Frost was hardly a saint. Once I sat next to his daughter on a plane. She looked just like him, with blue eyes and white hair. I never asked her who she was or about her rift of long years with her father. We just chatted.

Two boys from the suite across the hall, Joe and Ronnie, were Jewish, and they were from New Orleans and Memphis. Their parents like most upper-class southern Jews were charming and very aristocratic. I don't remember if we ever talked about religion or ethnicity among ourselves. In fact, few of us went to church, but we did go to Battelle Chapel to hear great preachers like Reinhold Niebuhr, Paul Tillich, and James Pike. Charlie was an Episcopalian, and we used to go across the street to an Episcopal church called "Smoky Steve's." There were lots of whistles, bells, and incense. The students who flocked there and to the martinis after Sunday Evensong were "mannerist" in their imitation Englishness. That was not for me. I liked the church but had too many doubts about religion to join up.

There were so many things that I did not know about. For example, the English D'oyly Carte Opera Company, dedicated to Gilbert and Sullivan, performed at the Shubert Theater in New Haven before the troop went to New York. Our college master invited the company to dinner, and afterward, they sang. I have never forgotten one of the three little maids from the *Mikado*. Margaret Mitchell, as Yum Yum, in the opera was handsome in a vibrant English way, and I still think of her that way after all these years.

I took all the requisite premed courses but learned the most from literature courses. One class in the philosophy of religion was especially interesting, but at the time, I was not sure why. I had studied T. S. Eliot in an introductory course and went to New York to see his play *The Cocktail Party*. The play had a powerful impact on me. The central character, Celia, was reaching for a spiritual experience, perhaps martyrdom, which I felt but could not understand. Clearly something was going on within me that was beyond any tutelage I had as a Presbyterian.

Psychology courses were often disappointing, because they were dry and formalistic in an effort to seem as scientific as possible, which made me very skeptical. The professors avoided saying much about human personality, because it was hard to study scientifically. Of course, this eventually drew me to psychiatry. I did not know anything about anthropology but wished that I had, because in my later work, I learned that one had to understand the culture or subculture of patients in order to treat them properly.

Our four years at Yale were, as the alma mater "Bright College Years" says, "the shortest, gladdest years of life," and indeed, they were wonderful, particularly "for the friendships formed at Yale." We came as boys. We left as men, still unseasoned, still uncertain, but moving in the general directions we chose. We would not find a plateau to run on until we were thirty. I decided to go to medical school at Cornell in New York City, partly because I loved New York. Don't ask me why I turned down Harvard. Cornell was smaller, and that appealed to me. The Korean War had begun, and some of my friends were being drafted; however, I luckily received a medical deferment. George was going to study history at Johns Hopkins so that he could escape the draft. The army grabbed Clay, though, because he was footloose.

The prospect of med school equally excited and frightened me. I had been a pretty good science student, but the idea of healing people drew me to the profession. Although I wasn't too sure what psychiatrists did, I knew that understanding human personality interested me. In retrospect, I realize now that my early family life caused me to reach in that direction. When I lost my mother, I lost a sustaining hand that would have always helped and supported me. I turned to my father and then lost him to Kitty. Dad was good to me, especially as I grew older and needed practical advice, but he was also absorbed in his medical practice and his marriage. I worked so hard in my professional years, because I desperately wanted my father's approval. I realized much later that I had always felt that his approval was conditional on my success. This gave my work a certain obsessive quality that I was able to overcome only through self-analysis many years later. It did, however, make me successful professionally, but it exacted a price, too.

I learned to look after myself. Indeed, that is perhaps the root of some of my initiative and search for originality. I had turned my anger against myself, and it showed in a year or two when my poor grades starting appearing in school. By the time I got to high school, my studies turned me on again. I was strongly motivated to succeed for my own sake and for no one else. But there was an emotional void within me, a yearning for something that I could not put my finger on. My interests in literature and then religion pointed a way for which I was reaching. My occasional bouts of insomnia, as I discovered later in my psychoanalysis, were efforts to keep negative feelings buried. The capacity for hard, disciplined work reinforced all of this.

My fellow medical students were a varied lot. In the fall of the first year, I did not understand why students would wish each other "happy new year." I knew little about Rosh Hashanah. There were a few women who were clearly "brains" and lots of guys from all kinds of backgrounds and regions. First-year students were idealistic that we were in a noble profession, but we had no idea of the stresses and strains ahead. Our idealism was eventually dampened but not extinguished. The gradual enhancement of our skills gave us self-confidence that we had something to offer. A doctor's inside track to the human comedy provided a steady realism, which was in itself sustaining. Failure was our strongest fear. Older students told us that the faculty taught by fear, and the only protection was increased competence.

Seeing New York Hospital, a large white temple on the east side of Manhattan, was like seeing the Taj Mahal for the first time. One felt small but proud to enter the temple. I shared a small suite in a dormitory with two Yale classmates: Roy, who wanted to be a surgeon, and Ben, who aspired to be a researcher. Neither one saw psychiatrists as "real" doctors. One just talked with people. How could that be medicine? It wasn't until useful drugs were developed that we would be accepted as doctors, and even then many abused their privilege and overprescribed drugs.

The faculty threw a torrent of work at us and did teach by fear. For example, six of us shared a cadaver, whom we named Barney Google. He was real and not real at the same time. We helped each other all the time, out of the wish to learn but also out of fear of our lab superviser who wore thick rubber-soled shoes and sneaked up on us without warning. He would stick his pick into Barney and interrogate us about Barney's body parts. We were ignorant and shamed. We took turns looking out for him, but he was usually too quick for us.

There was so much work that we were in a trap. We could not learn everything in the lectures, labs, and reading. We had to fasten onto the essentials as best we could. They wanted us to find relationships, which was not easy to do. It was only with pathology that things began to fall into place. We began to see patients in the latter two years. I loved pathology, because the medical history, lab findings, and the gross anatomical and microscopic findings could be wrapped into an understanding of diseases and possible remedies.

The work was so hard that one could not last without certain capabilities beyond smarts—the ability to sleep whenever needed because one never got enough sleep, a sense of humor, and above all, the strong desire to be a doctor. It was not just fear of failure. We really wanted to reach the goal and practice medicine, even though we only understood little about it then.

We were completely cut off from the world, except for drinking beer, seeing nurses, and watching baseball. On off days, we went to the ball park where the Yankees, Giants, or Dodgers played. Nurses were everywhere. Most of us, including myself, were ignorant about sex. But some friendly nurses were only too ready to initiate one into the mysteries. They were nice girls who just wanted to have fun, much like the girls I had known from the other side of town in high school.

I started to attend the Episcopal Church of the Epiphany, which was near the hospital. Communion and the Book of Common Prayer drew me in. It was so different from the meetinghouse character of the Presbyterian church. Something transcendent was taking place. It was the cross rather than the rooster that was on our church at home.

The first summer after med school, I went home and did lab tests for my father. George was home from Johns Hopkins, and we discovered a common interest. I wanted to take a good medical history of a patient, and he wanted to understand the biography of individuals, institutions, and countries. We had to separate knowns from unknowns and search for the best, always incomplete, information that we could find. Oral history intrigued George, and that was not far from what I wanted to learn.

The course in clinical medicine in the second year taught us to take a clinical history. The most important point was to listen to the patient and not ask yes or no questions. One wanted to know the medical history of a patient and the medical histories of parents and grandparents. We were to encourage the patients to talk about their lives, their work, and their home environments. The clinical reports that we submitted were usually returned heavily edited with red pencil. We also went on rounds with doctors and residents, standing in the back row where we could barely see. Even as they rewarded competence and struck more fear into hearts, doctors grilled the residents about patients. Some professors were dramatic. One presented a bloody sheet and asked the students to estimate how much blood was on the sheet. The guesses were much too high then, as he demonstrated by pouring a small vial of blood on a clean sheet.

I felt more confident that I could actually become a physician after the second year and volunteered to work in a clinic in south India that summer. We lived in dormitories at a site between Bangalore and Mysore in southern India and assisted doctors, nurses, and pharmacists, all who were providing primary care. Complex cases were sent to hospitals. We tested vision and provided glasses, operated for glaucoma, pushed out kidney stones, gave pills for malaria, and taught mothers how to keep their babies healthy and what to feed them. Public health doctors worked with local officials on clean water and waste disposal. I gradually realized that these people had lived and worked as they had for thousands of years. One had to understand their customs in order to treat them. We talked to them through Indian doctors. Very few had ever been to school, but they were still intelligent. They listened carefully and were grateful for the help. The clinic's work had been negotiated carefully by Indian doctors with local councils. There was a kind of oligarchical "democracy" in every village.

It was a beautiful country with green fields and tall, swaying trees. Everyone except very small children worked in the fields. People were thin, even though food was available, and they all worked very hard. Hindu temples throughout the countryside were filled at all times of the day and night with people praying to family gods in the pantheon of Hindu polytheism. I learned that all life was understood according to the great Hindu cycle of birth, death, rebirth, and the purification of the soul. One could only purify one's soul as one moved through the endless cycle of birth and rebirth.

The monsoon came in August, and people ran out into the rain, laughing and dancing at the rebirth of life. I would never forget India and would return often. We finally had to pack up and go home to a hot New York City for our two clinical years. We were then beginning to feel like real doctors for the first time, because we were seeing patients in rotation on different services. I came to loathe surgeons, because I was clumsy and hated to be yelled at. Obstetrics, pediatrics, and the medical subspecialties did not appeal to me. It was to be either internal medicine or psychiatry, and the first was the best path to the second. At that time, most medical students had no use for psychiatry. They did not regard talk therapy, which then dominated psychiatry, as medicine. They were also afraid of patients with chronic illnesses like schizophrenia. Psychoanalysts led most psychiatry departments in those years, and the drugs that would later treat chronically ill patients were not yet available. And talk therapy did not usually help them.

In the public clinic, we were the first people to see patients who suffered from various ailments. Residents then managed the cases, and we met with them to test our diagnoses. It was a valuable education, especially when faculty members corrected all of us. We enjoyed the patients in their variety. One beautiful movie star, usually filled with alcohol and drugs, came to the emergency room almost every Saturday night. Students and residents drew lots for Saturday night duty. The head resident in psychiatry brought a schizophrenic woman to grand rounds one day, and she told us that a man came into her room every night. The doctor repeatedly asked what he looked like, and she would not answer. Finally, she blurted out, "He looks just like you." She was quickly removed amid hilarious laughter.

I stayed on for a fifth year as an intern, and in the fall of 1957, I began looking for residencies in psychiatry. Interviews with heads of departments were straightforward, but were they peering into my psyche, looking for slips of the tongue or nervous twitches? They always asked why I wanted to be a psychiatrist. My standard answers were that I was interested in personality and wanted to help people in pain. I was accepted at Harvard, Columbia, and Cornell, and I eventually chose Harvard. Then the doctor draft intervened. My draft board at home would defer me only for one year at Harvard, so I signed up to join the Public Health Service as an officer to serve my residency at the National Institutes of Health outside Washington. I would begin after my first year of residency.

CHAPTER 3

George
Education in Life, 1948–1957

Washington and Lee was beautiful with its green lawns, brick walks, and Georgian buildings with white pillars. My mother was in a state of rapture. The students looked like "such gentlemen," she gushed. Dad took it all in with amusement. I felt at home and had no difficulty pledging Phi Delt, even though I was shy, because my father and grandfather had been Phi Delts at UNC. The boys, most of whom were southerners, looked like John, Clay, and me, and their parents looked like my parents. It was all civility and feeling comfortable. It wasn't long before we got to meet girls from Sweet Briar, Mary Baldwin, Hollins, and Randolph Macon. All of them looked like our sisters or mothers.

Student life revolved around friendship, girls, and parties, which were often rolled into one. The courses were well taught, and students were mildly interested; however, there was little intellectual life. Most boys expected to join their fathers or uncles in comfortable enterprises back home. I enjoyed my courses, and by sophomore year, I found some very good history and political science professors with whom I could have long talks. I liked both American and English history, and I was fascinated by southern history; however, research on the progressive movement and the New Deal was flowering, and I wanted to join in. I didn't tell my mother about this, though.

The four years passed quickly. In my senior year, I wrote an honors thesis on Harry Hopkins as a policy adviser and administrator in the New Deal and got my teeth into real research for the first time. As I considered graduate school, the most appealing place was Johns Hopkins, because it was strong in American history and political science. It was also smaller than Harvard or Columbia, the two best departments for American history in the country.

Departmental faculty members at Hopkins selected their own graduate students with the expectation that their choices would study with them.

My mentor, I hoped, would turn out to be Austin Riggs, an expert on the progressive movement and the New Deal, so I went up to Baltimore to see him in early winter. I saw an open door and looked in to see a man with floppy black hair and amused eyes.

"You're George Logan?"

"Yes, sir."

"Don't just stand there. Come in and tell me why you want to study history."

"Well, sir, I like American history, particularly biography."

"Why biography? Do you think that individuals matter in history? Is the study of individuals really history?"

I paused to think. "If history is narrative, then it must be seen through the lives of individuals."

Riggs's eyes flashed to show the crinkles around them. "What about economic and social history, the big sweeps in which individuals only reflect their times?"

"Well, even if individuals reflect historical forces, we need to know that. I just mean to say that I don't want to study history without people in it. My interest is the interaction of individuals and groups within their historical setting." I waited for his reaction.

"You've come to the right place," he said. "We can work together to study that puzzle. Are you ready for uncertainty?"

"Yes, sir. But ... I thought that historians aspired to reduce uncertainty."

"Fair enough. There are always gaps in knowledge, and our interpretations will necessarily vary. We can narrow the disagreements, but history is not a science. That is the excitement of it. Do you agree?"

I agreed and sailed home on a high cloud.

I looked for a place to live when I would return in September and found an apartment over a three-car garage in an expensive-looking house in Roland Park near the university. The apartment was comfortable with a bedroom, kitchen, and living room that could be converted into a study. It came with the owner, an attractive sixty-year-old widow with auburn hair and a wonderful figure. I was dazzled by her. Sheila Oates seemed very happy to have me, perhaps too happy.

As classes began, I was nervous. My fellow students were bright and full of themselves, but they were surely as nervous as I was. Once classes were under way, I could see that I was as smart as some and smarter than others. I seemed to have a feel for the complexity of historical interpretation, which may have been a sense of proportion, of how things fitted together. My two fields were American and English history with political science as an outside field. Professor Riggs and I went to town on twentieth-century American history, which I saw as a study of the rise, fall, and rise of progressive reform politics against the tapestry of strongly conservative anchors in our society. In short, I accepted a progressive theory of American history. Reform would always win over setbacks.

It wasn't until much later that I saw the limitations of this bias. I leaned to biography, loving Theodore Roosevelt despite his bombast, admiring Woodrow Wilson, who was hard to like very much, and then turning to the "happy warrior" FDR, who was a sphinx to say the least. I was less interested in Republican presidents, aside from TR, and it was only much later that I would see clearly Dwight Eisenhower and his strengths.

FDR fascinated me, because he was so hard to figure out. Oliver Wendell Holmes said that the new president had a "second-class intellect but a first-class temperament," by which I thought he meant a high spirit and optimism that would carry him through. That was certainly true, but Holmes missed the reality that FDR had a first-class political intelligence, sometimes today called "emotional intelligence." He could read people well, and experience had taught him how to manage and persuade others, when to press and when to hold back. This helped explain the seeming contradictions in his personality. He was a lion when politics were running in his favor and a fox who would temporize, sometimes endlessly, when conditions were unfavorable. His ideas and ideals were eloquent but often vague, giving him room to aim high or low as he judged best. His charm and ability as an actor drew people to him, but he was also an easy target for hatred because of his self-confident, perhaps even narcissistic, personality. He was secretive as he figured out his strategies and tactics. He used lieutenants as long as they were useful to him, but his interests and objectives were paramount.

I wanted to write about Roosevelt and the politics of the New Deal as one instance of progressive politics, detailing its weaknesses as well as its strengths. The New Deal was never radical. Punches were pulled again and again to stay in the political mainstream. The goal was to reform and protect capitalism while we moved gradually and incrementally in the direction of social welfare policies, but nowhere near a European welfare state. I decided that I wanted to focus on FDR's decision-making style, which embodied his contradictions, so I plunged in, reading the New Deal literature and biographies of Roosevelt through seminars and independent study.

I eventually hit on a dissertation topic of FDR and the Tennessee Valley Authority. He had conceived of a plan for an organization in the valley that would harness electric power, give technical assistance to farmers, including the manufacture of fertilizer, improve navigation and flood control, and introduce forestry conservation to seven states in the valley. He persuaded congress to create the authority, and a three-person board was instituted to run the TVA; however, FDR never told them what he had wanted. He just let them fight it out, and fight they did. Any idea of a master plan was lost in practice, and I wanted to understand why and what eventually emerged.

My father had given me a 1949 Ford, the best car I have ever had. It would get me to the valley and back, as well as to interviews and the Roosevelt Library at Hyde Park. But I had a problem. I was sleeping with my landlady, the seductive Sheila, and she was not happy about the idea of my being away from her.

The relationship had begun so easily and simply. In the early weeks of my first year, she invited me over for a drink, which often led to dinner. One thing led to another—hands touching, brushing past each other, her hand on my back as she handed me a drink. It was basic, downright physical attraction. I was convinced that she had seduced me, and I loved it. I was far too shy and inexperienced for any other explanation. I hated to leave her warm bed at night and go out to my cold garage. She was loving, sexy, funny, and smart. How could an innocent young man from a small town in the South resist? Sheila's grown-up son and daughter had no inkling of all this and seemed to like me.

I suspected that I was more dependent on her than she was on me. Yet when I told her that I would have to travel to do my research, she resisted. I was looking ahead, and she saw that she was going to lose me eventually. Perhaps I had taken her for granted as one did dessert after dinner.

"Why do you have to travel? Can't you do something here?"

"Not really," I said. "The research materials are in Knoxville."

"Will you be away a lot?"

"A few weeks at a time, and I can commute to Washington and the FDR Library on short trips."

"Still, I don't like it," she said.

She was still very attractive at sixty-two, but I could see then that I had taken advantage of her. My future was wide open, and hers was uncertain.

I began to hope that she would marry, even though it gave me a pang of jealousy. She had dated other men, and I had been jealous, fearing that she might sleep with them. I was learning that sex wasn't just a physical act. It was morally complicated, because feelings always intruded. We had become much more attached to each other than mere sexual recreation would suggest. She eventually learned to live with it as I hit the road, and our life together continued.

I very much enjoyed doing primary research, digging into archives and interviewing past and present TVA staff members, as well as the original and subsequent board members. Roosevelt had sought a wide compass for the authority and then watched the three directors fight for control. The chairman wanted to plan for the states, but the other two directors were more practical and wanted TVA to provide public power and assistance to farmers. FDR tilted in favor of planning, but as such hopes floundered, he swung toward the practical, throwing his weight to the mandated missions accordingly. His rhetoric reached for the skies, but in practice, the TVA became a bundle of separate missions with electric power as the dominant activity. The TVA reflected the New Deal in its anchoring of concrete programs, none of which came anything close to planning or comprehensiveness. The reins were held by the grand master in the White House. My dissertation was easily turned into a book about FDR but also about the halfway reforms of the New Deal, which were in no sense radical.

In 1956, I had to face the draft, but fortunately, I was able to serve six months at the Pentagon in military intelligence and then released to the reserves. I arrived at Brown University in September 1957 with a new doctorate degree. The history department was strong, and I soon realized that one was expected to write, publish, and also teach well. I taught two courses each semester, and I spent the first year writing lectures, preparing seminars, and turning my TVA study into a book. I saw Sheila on regular visits to Baltimore. We always kept in touch, and after I married and she was growing older, we became good friends. I never stopped loving her.

Brown University was on a hill overlooking the city of Providence, and the campus was surrounded by handsome Georgian houses. The town-gown relationships were much as they had been at Hopkins, with lots of connections among trustees and local nabobs and friendships of faculty members with mostly professional people in town. I saw little of this in my early years, because I was working very hard preparing for classes and revising the thesis for publication. It was pretty heady stuff, because secretaries and students called me "professor" in deference I had never received.

I began to feel like a grown-up, something you never feel in the tutelage of graduate school. I had a special status as professor, even though "assistant" still went before "professor." Of course, I knew that my future depended on how the real grown-ups in the department assessed me. I discovered that if one taught well, positive reputation filtered back to them, and things relaxed for me, because poor teaching usually meant no reappointment. A professor was given three initial years to prove himself as a teacher, and then he was given a second three-year appointment if his writing seemed promising. Then it was up or out with an extra year to find a job.

My classes went well. The students were smart, talkative, and willing to challenge each other. I learned that the best way to teach was to ask questions in both seminars and lectures. I posed questions about the material: Was the American Revolution simply a war for independence or a real revolution? What did that mean? Then I suggested different interpretations and let them have at it, even in lecture courses. The exams were not about having them repeat what *I* thought but about having them explain what *they* thought. Everyone liked stories, so I dramatized history through biography by bringing Hamilton, Madison, and Jefferson into the stories. I could do the same with Hoover, FDR, Truman, and Eisenhower. If a teacher loved his subject and showed his enthusiasm to the students, they would respond in kind.

I was always talking about the American democratic experience, particularly the nature of liberalism. I had been raised as a southern Democrat and had moved far beyond, but I was not sure how far. I could not conceive of being a Republican. The Republicans had been consistently wrong as a national party in their opposition to the New Deal, their isolationism, their crusades against communism at home and abroad, and their fundamentalist ideas of economics. I saw virtues in Eisenhower and so-called modern Republicans in regards to their moderation and practicality. My political ideas were borrowed from contemporary British Conservative Party ideas, which balanced free markets with a welfare state but rejected socialism. Democrats were sometimes naïve about human progress, and I valued, above all, a realism that accepted people as they were and understood the importance of acting with prudence and some skepticism about what the government could do.

My social life was limited during the first few years at the university. Most of my faculty peers were married, and wives didn't seem to like having bachelors around. Few young women were on the faculty. A "smart set" of young townspeople pretty much kept to themselves, and I had little in common with them in any case. They were very much rooted in kith and kin, who moved back and forth between the east side of Providence and summer houses at Sakonet Point on Narragansett Bay. A friend was once visiting Sakonet when he noticed that the names on the mailboxes were the same names as those in the Swan Point cemetery in Providence. That told me a lot about the city's upper class. I was thirty years old in 1960, appointed to a second three-year term, with one book under my belt and a promising future, but I was still lonely.

CHAPTER 4

Clay
Craft and Promise, 1948–1964

The University of Missouri in Columbia was not really foreign territory. Students from the North thought that they had gone South, and those from the South thought that they had gone North. The blend was happy—soft manners without many southern prejudices. The university was fairly ordinary; however, the journalism school was outstanding, and I was able to take the arts and sciences courses that I wanted. I enjoyed sinking my teeth into reporting, editing, and managing. I learned how to interview and write short, succinct sentences and avoid overwriting by using too many adjectives and adverbs. Clear writing reflected clear thinking. I learned to reduce complex subjects to readable prose.

I did not pay too much attention to social life; however, there were a lot of pretty girls to date, and I did my share of that. I gradually worked my way up and became an editor of the student daily newspaper, which took a lot of time, hurt my studies, and ensured that I would get little sleep. But the bug had bitten me. I was a reporter for life who thought that the "story" was all-important. You had to feel that way to track stories down.

For two summers, I worked as a police reporter for the *Chattanooga Times*. I remember what the editor said when he hired me: "I'm going to put you in the police districts. If you can do that well, you can cover the United Nations." It was great training to look for stories on the police blotter, find a story, and call it into the rewrite desk. I had to spell names correctly, get the middle initial, and—this always bothered me—tell the race of the key people in the story. It didn't always make it to the paper, but it did when it seemed relevant to the city editor.

My best story was taken off a police blotter. A twelve-year-old white boy had thrown himself off a cliff in a quarry while he had been shouting, "I can fly!" The other boys said that he had drunk a half pint of whiskey. I was curious and began to talk with some of the neighborhood boys, who led me to their mothers. The boy had begged several mothers to take him in to live with them. His father was in a TB sanitarium, and he was living with a stepmother who was a visiting nurse and seldom home. I found her in the early evening. She was not particularly sympathetic, seemingly having no feelings at all. I wrote the story through a rewrite man and got a byline the next morning. I had learned how to dig for a story.

The Korean War had begun in the summer of 1950, but those of us in college usually received deferments. John had gotten a deferment for medical school, and George had served briefly; however, I had been caught. I volunteered for the draft in the summer of 1952 and received a telegram from the president of the United States: "Greetings. Your Friends and Neighbors have selected you." Basic training was in September in the heat of Fort Jackson, South Carolina. I learned that I could walk ten miles with a full pack on my back and do other useful things. When I couldn't hit the target at the firing range, I discovered I needed glasses, which the army gave me. They were plain wire frames, but I wore them when I needed to. I looked like an old man wearing them.

I then graduated to signal school at Camp Gordon, Georgia. I liked Augusta; it was like home, and I met a nice girl named Polly in Milledgeville. But she was in college, and our lives had crossed at the wrong time. After I went off to Germany, we wrote to each other, but nothing developed. I still think about her and wonder where she is and what she's doing. She had been lost in the mist.

The large troop ship, the Simon Bolivar Buckner, took ten days to get to Bremerhaven on the Baltic Sea in Germany. The North Atlantic was freezing, and I was sick, threw up, and had KP for three days. Our bunk beds were stacked by three. Officers and their wives had cabins on the top levels, and we would sometimes go up to watch them walk their dogs on the front deck. I remember one wife telling her ugly little dog to "doo-doo" while her husband, a major, walked the dog in a circle. It would not "doo-doo," and the major looked very sheepish. Most draftees thought the army was ridiculous anyway, and this silliness confirmed it. The undertone of humor perhaps saved us from insanity. There were so many incompetent officers and noncoms that we college graduates could feel superior.

I was sent to Stuttgart to work in the seventh army message center. My greatest achievement was learning to roll my own cigarettes, filling the paper from a tobacco pouch, licking it smooth, and lighting one end. Some guys could do it with one hand, but I could not master it. It was a wonderful, if short, smoke. I never went back to it but appreciated the boys who taught me. They were not all southerners, but only the southerners chewed tobacco.

It's hard to forget some of those guys. I became good friends with a Negro from my state, Jerry Daniels, who was the only black person in the battalion. One of the friends in his platoon, Charlie Justice, was also from North Carolina. Charlie used to get angry when black soldiers brought German girls to the PX; however, when Jerry was knocked down by a guy from Brooklyn for no apparent reason, Charlie's anger boiled over, and he hit the guy in the hallway and knocked him down. No one was going to hurt his friend Daniels. It drove home a point about race in the South that I understood.

You learn a lot about Americans from the army. None of the boys was curious about Europe. The majority never left the base and wouldn't eat German bread, preferring the spongy American kind. They were very much rooted in the places where they had grown up and meant to return. They obeyed orders but hated the army. We were patriotic and cheered when we saw the Statue of Liberty in the New York harbor. There was a lump in my throat, which I have never forgotten.

The *Chattanooga Times* took me back as a general reporter. After a year there, I learned that the *Baltimore Morning Sun* was hiring, so I took myself to Baltimore and presented my clippings to Charles "Buck" Dorsey, the managing editor. He was white-haired and red-faced, and he had the sardonic look of a man who had seen and heard everything. He did not read the clippings I gave him, because, as he said, he had no openings, but he kept them. Two weeks later, his secretary called and offered me a job at ninety-three dollars a week. He may have read my clippings and talked with someone in Chattanooga, because I was put on the city desk as a reporter. I later read in Russell Baker's memoir that Dorsey had hired him the same way.

I found an apartment and fell into a routine of working from four until midnight, covering all kinds of stories. The paper was loaded with talent competing for top jobs in Baltimore, the large Washington bureau, and several foreign bureaus. We were proud to be there, because the paper was among the best, even though one editor called it "the best unread paper in America." It was wasted on Baltimore, but it was read in Washington and elsewhere. The local Hearst paper had a higher circulation.

There were lots of characters. One copy editor was a professor of philosophy at Hopkins who used his paycheck to play the horses. Another had been married three times and kept proposing to whichever young woman was the social editor. He wrote the cleanest prose I have ever seen. After work at midnight, we would go to Obrycki's and eat hard or soft shell crab and then wash it down with cold draft beer. We would go to the strip joints on the "Block" and appreciate the talent. I saw Blaze Starr, Dolores Del Rio, and Candy Barr, among others. They were terrific. The Belvedere Hotel had the most magnificent wooden bar beneath stained glass windows, and we loved to go there, as well as Miller Brothers.

We worked on weekends and saw little of the city by day. John was there for one year at Hopkins Hospital, and George was finishing his last year in graduate school. We saw each other when we could and wondered about the future. Each of us seemed to have a way up. John's future was the most secure, because he was a doctor. George hoped to get a job at a good university, and I hoped to be promoted within the paper. At that time, I never thought of looking for a newspaper job elsewhere. The *Sun* was the apex.

In the early years, I covered all kinds of stories, particularly the courts and local government. The courts were much more lenient with blacks convicted of murder than they were with whites, because the blacks were not regarded as responsible as whites. In this instance, their race helped them. A police captain once told me that he would rather deal with black people than white hillbillies. The black would go home and go to bed after he shot someone, whereas the hillbilly might go on a tear and shoot someone else. I covered the police department's vice squad as they arrested prostitutes and gamblers and then covered them again when they were arrested for taking bribes. I learned that anyone brought before the court needed a lawyer, because to be without one was to be at the mercy of the police and prosecutors. The lawyers who hung around the courts to pick up clients were important.

Eventually, I moved to local government and covered colorful Mayor D'Alesandro at his home in Little Italy. The city desk told me to see him and ask why he had bought the building next door to his home. Was it for an office? I said to him, "My desk would like to know why you bought the building next door."

He looked at me for a moment and then leaned down as if to listen to his desk. Then he said, "My desk tells your desk to go to hell." We both laughed, and we shared some small talk before I left. He was as wily as he could be.

By 1960, I had become a good reporter, but the excitement was fading. I didn't make enough money and didn't like working at night. Then I met Molly through some friends. We were the same age and hit it off immediately. Our conversations moved back and forth like soft butter. She wrote about Maryland history and architecture and worked as a consultant to several historical societies and museums. I could tell that she was happy, because she smiled and laughed a lot, but she was also a good listener.

After lots of lunches and midweek dates, we just naturally fell into marriage. John and George were in the wedding, and she got along wonderfully with them. In later years, I often thought that they liked her better than me. We moved into a town house in Bolton Hill, a home that we still own today. I began to write a column about life in the city, and Alice came along after two years.

In May 1965, Dorsey called me into his office and said, "You're going to the London bureau."

"I am?"

"Don't you want to go?"

"Sure, but I have to ask Molly," I said.

"Ask her and let me know in a few days."

"Yes, sir. How long will I be there?"

"How the hell should I know?" he said. "Maybe five years."

"Yes, sir."

Then, a new phase of our lives began.

CHAPTER 5

John
Finding One's Way, 1956–1961

I reported for work at Massachusetts General Hospital in July 1956 and soon realized how little I knew about psychiatry. I was assigned to a ward in the hospital but was afraid to talk with any patients because I felt so ignorant. The head resident chaired the meeting of first-year residents with a senior psychiatrist often sitting in. We were to present the cases of our four patients for general discussion, and our diagnoses would compete with others. Each of us hoped to be convincing; we could not afford to look clueless. We also had lectures about psychiatry supplemented by grand rounds with senior doctors and patients.

Our work was not nearly as coherent or academic as that of clinical psychologists, but our methods may have suited the discipline that was based on cases rather than theories. Our task was to learn to spot symptoms and invent remedies. The trouble was that symptoms did not always guarantee accurate diagnoses. We might mislabel patients, which could lead to false remedies. However, the emphasis on therapy for individuals permitted us to change tactics if necessary. I decided early on that the best strategy was to ask the patients questions about their feelings and get them to talk rather than try to find an appropriate label to slap on them.

For instance, Ben was a very depressed man who was also gay. Most diagnoses would have focused on his sexual identity, because at that time, homosexuality was believed to be an illness. I just asked him to tell his story. He was fifty years old, born in Boston, and had gone to New York City with the hope of becoming a dance band vocalist. That didn't pan out, so he went into public relations for an airline and was eventually transferred to Los Angeles. He had a happy life for a number of years and found a partner as well as good friends.

But everything had come apart two years ago. When the airline denied his request for a raise, he resigned only to discover that no one wanted to hire him at his age. His partner abandoned him, and he returned home to a married sister who did not know that he was gay. He found a job selling clothes in a men's store, but diabetes in his legs made it impossible for him to stand for any length of time.

When I first saw Ben in the hospital, he was filled with self-pity and anger. He was a member of AA, but his bleak view of life kept him from attending very often. He seemed to have a very weak ego and a low sense of self-esteem, and he depended on others to help him. Yet he had just his sister, who could be of little help. I decided that his being gay was not the cause of his problems, except that he had always felt himself to be an outsider. The difficulties of life had overwhelmed him. He was caught in a trap that he had constructed for himself in large part.

His priest from St. Matthew's Catholic Church visited him regularly. Even though he did not go to church anymore, he remembered happy early years there. One day, I asked Ben if there might be any volunteer work for him at the church. He then asked Father Ruggles, who suggested that Ben help serve Communion, answer the telephone, and do some filing, for which he would be paid. However, the priest added a condition: Ben's attitude would have to be more cheerful.

Ben eventually tried doing the job after we released him. He was now in a supportive environment. The work was easy, and his priest simply ignored his gay life, which was not active anyway. I began to see from Ben's case how people differed in their capacity to overcome adversity. His sense of self-esteem was not strong enough for him to help himself by will alone.

I later wondered whether I should have made the intervention or not, and I eventually took the question to my supervisor, because we were not supposed to intervene in the lives of patients. He listened and said what I had done was okay. I had only made a suggestion to him based on my diagnosis. Ben had approached the priest; it would have been a mistake to do anything more that made him dependent on my actions.

The key to good therapy was finding the conflict that caused the symptoms and focusing on the defenses raised against it. We hold back pain by denial, repression, projection on to other people or incidents that we blame, and physical symptoms like insomnia and supposed illness. My job was to dig into the symptoms to find the underlying conflicts and pull them into consciousness.

One did not recover suppressed memories but explored the buried feelings that lead to symptoms. The patient must then work through such feelings in his everyday life to clear his emotions of them. A psychoanalyst might take months for feelings and insights to surface, but I preferred a more active role in which I would ask the patient to confront defenses and work through them. The problem is that one may not give the patient enough time to come up with his own insights, but then he was not on the couch for years.

Psychotic patients, such as schizophrenics and manic depressives, were not amenable to talk therapy, perhaps because their problems were more physiological in origin. Effective drugs for them were years away. Therapy could counsel them in practical problems of living and perhaps acceptance of their illnesses, but it fell far short of effective treatment.

One of my patients rejected treatment. She was not hospitalized but came into the clinic. Understanding borderline personalities had been difficult. These people bottled up their fears, however they arose, by blaming everyone except themselves. They were in such denial that they were not open to therapy. This woman was smart and capable, but anything that she took as criticism caused an explosion and usually the loss of a job. Her family members kept thinking that she had become reasonable at times, but she fooled them again and again by outbursts and failures. They finally decided to have little to do with her. She would see me when they insisted, but she wanted me to give her sympathy rather than therapy. I could not help her until she admitted her need for help.

Psychiatric nurses often knew the hospitalized patients better than the doctors, because they saw more of them, and patients found it easier to talk to nurses rather than men or women in white coats. I learned a great deal from the nurses. My first year in the hospital was a good start, but I was well aware that I had much more to learn. We learned all the labels and the standard treatments, but the art laid in matching the two or seeing beyond labels and remedies to the individuality of the situations. It was no different from other branches of medicine, which relied on science as a point of departure for art.

I moved to Bethesda, Maryland, in the summer of 1958 to continue my residency for two years at NIH. I was to treat patients in a clinic and help senior psychiatrists with their research projects. I lived in a town house in Glover Park on the edge of Georgetown, with two internists, Duncan and Peter, who were also at NIH.

My hours were regular, and for the first time in years, I could have a private life. There were plenty of single girls with jobs all over town, so I did not have to wait long to meet someone. Mary was at home in

Washington, just having graduated from Smith, and she was a cub reporter for the *Washington Star*. One Sunday, we were both invited by friends to a farm in Virginia. I did not know Mary at all. As we sat beside a pond and talked, I saw that she was delightful. Her animated face and intelligent eyes complemented her quick mind and sense of humor. I called and asked her for lunch the next week. In due course, we began to date, but it was very clear that she was not interested in commitment. We had fun together, and I knew that she liked me but presumed no further. I did want to marry her. Who would not? But we never discussed it.

I remember taking her to the Russian Embassy in the fall, right after the Soviets invaded Hungary. Someone at work had given me the tickets. None of the Western embassies sent people, but there were lots of freeloading Latin Americans. The food and vodka were wonderful. We went up the stairs and shook hands with the ambassador and his wife. He looked like a professional wrestler in a fancy uniform. I noticed that his eyes fastened on Mary and followed her as far as they could go down the line. We also met Paul Robeson and his family. They wanted to talk about how he was not a Communist, and as a reporter tried to interview him, he brushed the reporter aside, saying that he preferred to talk with us.

Mary and I had a falling out in February. She won a part in an amateur musical comedy and was very absorbed in rehearsals, often practicing on the weekends. I was jealous and wanted her for myself, which annoyed her to no end. I did not acknowledge my jealous feelings, and I was not even aware of them back then. I was immature about women and paid a price for my behavior. She sensed my resentment, and when I showed my boredom at the cast party after the performance, she got mad and stayed that way. She rejected my requests for dates, and things sputtered to an end. She was a thoroughbred, highly sensitive and independent, and even though I was lots of fun and interesting—or so I thought—I was also an adolescent when it came to girls.

I rebounded fast. My housemate Duncan was on the verge of engagement to Elizabeth, a beautiful woman from the West. Her housemate, Rachel, was a good-looking girl from Seattle, a woman to whom I had paid no attention until we met one Saturday on Connecticut Avenue. After just a few words, I saw her differently. She had high cheekbones, green eyes, and blonde hair. On impulse, I called and asked for a date, and one thing led to another after that. She was a Republican, which I overlooked, who worked for a Midwestern Republican senator. I was finishing my first year at NIH, and we talked of marriage. She was open to it but began to equivocate during our discussions. After some questioning, I finally pulled the story out of her.

"A few years ago, I went out with a bachelor " _____" she said. "Our relationship ended, as do all his romances, but I cannot forget him. I must leave Washington to forget him and will go back to Seattle to do that."

"For how long?"

"I don't know."

I was incredulous. I asked myself Freud's question: What did women really want? Freud never answered the question, and I didn't have an answer, either.

I drove her to the National Airport on a hot July morning. Everything was up in the air. It seemed she was going into a void, and indeed, she was. I had the worst night of my life. I could not sleep, and I was in mental pain, feeling helplessly adrift as if I had lost my entire world. I had never felt such loss and despair. I did not recognize it at the time, but I was feeling the pain of the loss of my mother, which I had never permitted myself to experience.

I went to work, but during a break, I talked with the head of my clinic and asked about going into psychoanalysis. It was a question that I would face anyway as a psychiatrist in training, so I grabbed the nettle. I had not been sure that I wanted to be an analyst and sit and listen to people all day long; however, therapy of some kind was necessary for my work, and I just plunged in. I would have to borrow the money to pay the fees.

That week, I met Dr. Peter Dodge. He fit my idea of an analyst, plain and soft-spoken. I sat in a chair until he finally got me on the couch so that I would talk freely. It was never easy. Analysts asked about your current feelings, problems, and troubles on the assumption that they were manifestations of older, unresolved issues. If they were not, you didn't need analysis; you needed short-term therapy. It was not long before Rachel and my mother and my pain over the loss of both were joined. My father and stepmother were soon in the stew as my anger poured out. I felt the loss of my mother deeply for the first time. I missed her now because I wanted a hand at my back, but she was not there. Every hurdle in life and work had been that much harder because she was not there. My father had deserted me—or so I thought—and good as he was, he also abandoned me.

In due course, my deep ambivalence about women surfaced. I idealized them, as I did my mother, but I feared them as well, my stepmother being the negative case. I was anything but confident with them. My experiences with Mary and Rachel and my responses to loss became clear. Dodge and I spent more than a year for five days a week working through many things, including my feelings about psychiatry and medicine. In the spring of the second year, I was offered a head residency at Johns Hopkins medical school and wanted to take it. I could still work with Dodge on my off days and evenings, because his office was in Maryland just outside Washington.

At Hopkins, my job as head resident was to oversee the other residents, assign doctors to patients, and test my skills with the assessments of senior psychiatrists. My correspondence with Rachel just dropped off. She made the excuse that I could not marry while I was still in training.

Clay was then at the *Baltimore Sun*. George was doing research at Hopkins, and Duff, my Yale roommate, was in banking. When our schedules permitted, we would eat together at Obrycki's, a dumpy little place with wonderful crabs, which they dumped on tables, and we would wash down the food with pitchers of cold draft beer. We were all lonely, dating when we could, but nothing was clicking.

In the spring, I called Mary, and we dated some that summer. In June, we went to New York and searched for apartments, because I was going back to Cornell and she was moving to the city. I moved in July, and she had planned on coming in September; however, I did not call her for two months. Don't ask me why. I was settling into my new job. During that time, Duff met and married a beautiful girl from Virginia. I was in their wedding in a small Virginia town. Her parents owned a large house in the middle of town. Her family was graciously southern, but the family friends we met were very sharp-eyed men and elaborately courteous women.

As I walked into the big house before the wedding, I met Mary, who had come there as the bride's friend. She looked at me in the most skittish way.

"Why haven't you called me?" she said in an accusing tone.

"I don't know. I just didn't."

"That's an insult. We were friends."

"I thought that we were more than friends," I said.

"Not if you don't call me."

I could never win with her. After she moved to New York, I saw her a few times, but it trailed off. I didn't know why. Perhaps she was more than I could handle, and I saw that as a compliment to her. She was mercurial, and I needed consistency.

CHAPTER 6

George
Politics in Universities, 1957–1975

There were few women were on the faculty in those days, but I had noticed an interesting assistant professor in English named Peggy Ellis. Luckily, both of us were invited by students on the same night to have dinner in their dormitory. The housemother had no interest in either of us; however, we knew how to show off for the students, and it was fun. So we began a courtship of cleverness. We began to talk of marriage in the spring of our first year at Brown. She was a student of English Romantic poetry with a doctorate from Harvard. Her father was a stockbroker in Philadelphia, and her mother was president of the garden club and also an avid bridge player. Peggy loved them but was in a quiet rebellion against their conventionality. We were married in the summer of 1959. My mother would have preferred a southern girl, but we all got along fine.

We both had to win tenure if we were to stay at Brown and remain together. Peggy had published a well-regarded book on Keats and was now working on Byron. My book on the TVA had done well, and I was deep into a book on the Reorganization Act of 1939, in which FDR had created the White House Office and the Executive Office of the President.

Each of us won tenure in 1964 after our second books were published. We had to teach well in order to get a promotion at Brown, and although it was hard work, the students were good and a joy to teach. As I was looking for my next project, Peggy began to have epiphanies of sorts as she was swept up into women's studies. There had been plenty of work on Jane Austen, George Eliot, and Virginia Woolf, so critics reinterpreted these greats with feminist insights, discovered new neglected women authors, or applied feminist theory to male authors. Peggy also began to militate for separate women's studies programs or even departments, and she became very active in the affirmative action movement, recruiting women for the Brown faculty. She was often in the middle of several fights at Brown about tenure decisions that had usually gone against women. I was quiet about these things and tried to be sympathetic, although I was not a crusader by temperament.

And then the war came. I had thought that the Korean War was necessary as a limited conflict and initially saw the role of the United States in Vietnam in the same light. Gradually, it dawned on me that we had intruded into a civil war between North and South Vietnam, one in which we had few stakes. We had pursued the containment of communism far beyond the necessities. My authorities here were George Kennan and Reinhold Niebuhr, who had warned against the distortion of American crusades that reached beyond the national interest. This was different from critiques from the Left, which saw imperialist foreign policy serving capitalism and American militarism. In my view, our crusade was grounded in our nationalist universalism, which we used to see the world within our own national image.

I could never understand why students attacked the university in their opposition to the war. ROTC was banished, and the CIA could not interview students. I thought neither action was justified. Civilian politicians initiated the war, and it had wide public support at first. Then the military became a scapegoat.

Peggy was against the war from the beginning. I kept quiet, and I did not go to antiwar rallies with her. One night after we returned from a party with lots of radical talk, she called me a pig.

"Why did you do that?" I asked.

"Oh, I don't know. You're just so conservative."

I didn't know what she meant. I was a New Deal liberal, a southern advocate for civil rights policies who had had his consciousness raised by Martin Luther King, Jr.

"You don't do anything," she said. "What have you done to recruit women for the history faculty?" She hurled these words at me.

I did not reply, because I had done nothing. Affirmative action by law was just beginning to affect universities. We hired a woman that year, but we were denounced by a federal administrator who visited Brown departments, because we had not had a search pledging affirmative action. She had called the department chairman to an office she was occupying, putting him on the carpet, and among other scalding charges, she wanted to know why we had not looked for Puerto Rican candidates, because "they want to get off the island," as she said.

During the 1968 presidential election, I voted for Hubert Humphrey, but Peggy voted for Bob Gregory, the black comedian. Politics was poisoning our marriage. President Nixon sent American and South Vietnamese troops into Cambodia in the spring of 1970 to destroy North Vietnamese "sanctuaries for weapons and soldiers." The campuses erupted, and there was a terrible incident at Kent State University in which national guardsmen shot and killed student demonstrators.

The faculty senate, of which I was a member, met and debated actions against Nixon that the university should take. Antiwar male hormones were aroused in anger against Nixon, because he seemingly had widened the war. Strong advocates proposed sending a faculty delegation to meet with Henry Kissinger at the White House to express their opposition to Nixon's actions. I argued that doing so would politicize the university, thus destroying its very foundation. Naïve statements were made about the German universities' quiescence before Hitler, as if the universities could have prevented Hitler's coming to power. I was shouted down, and a delegation to see Kissinger was named.

After the Senate meeting, the full faculty met in the largest hall on campus to debate whether or not students should be excused from final exams in order to campaign against Nixon and the war. The debate was piped out to students on the lawn through loudspeakers. There was no real debate about the question. Denunciations of Nixon's actions dominated. One very nice professor of German was howled down when he suggested that the president might have known what he was doing. Nixon's explanation, given many years later, was that he was trying to stop attacks that were delaying the departures of American troops from Vietnam under the policy of gradually handing the war over to local forces. Either way, the students were excused from exams. I had seldom seen such mass hysteria.

A week later, Peggy and I went to Stanford, where I gave a talk to the history department. It had to be held in the chairman's home, because the graduate students would not go on campus. Some faculty members and students, including a friend of mine, skipped the talk in order to campaign against Nixon. Students had thrown rocks at large plate glass windows in the center of the campus and cracked them, so they were held together by some tape that looked like giant Band-Aids.

At a dinner that evening at a friend's house, Peggy said, thinking of the more moderate Brown students, that we should try to understand them. My friend immediately responded and practically shouted that students were gangsters who should be arrested. Peggy avoided what could have become a shouting match but later told me in no uncertain terms that I should have defended her.

This was the atmosphere when I celebrated my fortieth birthday in October 1970. We were growing apart and had no children, so there was little family glue to hold us together. Peggy was in her element at Brown, even though student and faculty radicalism was fairly mild compared to that in the best public universities in the Midwest and on the West Coast.

I was still uncomfortable because the political climate on campus was naïvely radical. It was clear that the public, in large numbers, would have to turn against the war and that Congress would act, which eventually happened in 1975, with President Ford vainly trying to help South Vietnam militarily in the face of congressional refusal.

Peggy still had plenty to be angry about, but in 1974, she calmed down enough to accompany me to California at the Center for Advanced Study in the Behavioral Sciences in Palo Alto, high in the hills above Stanford. She would have time to do her own work as well, a study of American women radicals. She had moved half-time to American studies and women's studies, and this was to be her fresh scholarly adventure.

My new project dealt with political ideology in American history. I was considering whether or not there was a centrist liberalism in American beliefs that had spurned socialism and lacked the aristocratic conservatism of European societies. Perhaps we were individualists, whether of the capitalist or progressive variety, who had not carried the Right and Left poles of English politics with us in our migrations. I saw a large American middle ground in which Left and Right strands argued about freedom and equality, all within the traditional language of English liberalism. There was a rhetorical battle, because the differences were so small. Standing in the center was a pragmatism that sought practical remedies without resorting to rhetorical fierceness. I pursued this analysis during the year and wrote a short book on American ideology that admirers regarded as accurate and critics dismissed as oversimplifying our politics. Peggy did not like it at all.

I did not mind that Peggy was radical, but her intolerance got my goat. She continually told me that I was a stick-in-the-mud for not marching and protesting. I was a Democrat and opposed to Nixon. Why didn't I get out there and protest? I was attacked because I was opposed to the university's boycotting California grapes when Cesar Chavez was leading strikes against giant farmers on the West Coast. My history department colleagues were also sticks-in-the-mud, except for a few of the younger members, but she told them what she thought of them which was painful for me.

Our day-to-day relationship soured until she finally moved out. In retrospect, I think that temperament divided us more than politics. I was a determined moderate, and she needed causes. My affection for her had dimmed, because her abuse of me had increased, and I am sure that she found me dull back then. We could have known none of these things at the outset of our marriage. We had a quick no-fault divorce. My mother was upset about the divorce, but she had never liked Peggy anyway.

I went into a dry period in the late 1970s, writing a few essays about American radicalism, Right and Left, and looking for a new project that would let me escape that old refrain once and for all.

CHAPTER 7

Clay
The Craftsman at Work, 1965–1970

We went to London in June with our little girl, Alice, and found a detached town house in Hampstead, only a few tube spots from the *Sun* office. Once we had settled in, we began to enjoy the delights of London's cultural life: the Old Vic and Royal Shakespeare theater companies, the symphonies and operas, and the sweetness of English life in tea rooms, parks, and pubs among ordinary people. Our daughter, Alice, went to a nursery school in Hampstead. The children would be a whirlwind on the playground until a teacher emerged to ring a big bell to get them into line. Their mothers would kiss them as if they were never going to see them again, and off they would go. It was gentle discipline without orders. Alice spoke with an English accent during those days.

I had a secretary and one assistant who could be called a legman, except that she was a smart young Englishwoman named Samantha. I eventually lost her to the *Guardian*, which was great for her and bad for me. My job was to cover parliamentary debates, particularly in the House of Commons, and use the access the *Baltimore Sun* could then command with the ministries and 10 Downing Street. I also talked regularly with business and labor leaders, all kinds of interest groups and citizen groups, as well as academics and public intellectuals.

I traveled around Britain seeking stories and getting a feel for the country. It was great fun to have an entire country as a beat instead of one assignment, but of course, I had to pick my shots carefully. I figured that my readers were less interested in parliamentary politics than in major stories about British government and politics and important trends in British society. I say "Britain," but England was really my beat, except for the occasional story from the Celtic fringe.

In 1965, English society was in ferment. The economy was sluggish, and business-labor conflicts were awful. The new Labour government, only a year old, was searching for new forms of economic "planning" in which business and labor would be involved and finding it difficult, because the weak pound required tight fiscal policies. Britain had spurned the Common Market and was later rejected for membership when it applied. There was much social criticism about the dated character of English life: the class system, the lack of modern management ideas, the amateurism of the national civil service, the old-fashioned character of the ancient universities and the "public" schools, which were misnamed private schools, and the traditionalism of the professions. The Edwardian institutions, which had been the glory of England, were derided as being antiquated and among the causes of English economic decline. Labor unions were militant, because manufacturing was not productive. Labour was also hampered by rigid, outworn socialist ideologies and militant labor leaders from the past.

The economic pie was growing smaller. Harold Wilson, the Labour prime minister, talked grandly of "modernization" and of replacing "the man in the cloth cap with the man in the white coat." There were all sorts of ideas about economic planning in companionship with industry, but the weak pound and balance of payments crises in which Britain spent more than it earned forced the government to balance government budgets with limited public expenditures.

Harold Wilson led a Labour Party that was divided between socialists who wanted to see the government run the economy through nationalized industries and moderates who wanted to use the government to stimulate modernization of industry through new technology and better private management. His cabinet, parliament, and the nation were split along those lines. He picked his fights carefully, for example, convening the Fulton Commission that recommended the reform of the higher civil service in terms of moving from the well-educated generalists of the past to people with management and specialist skills. Experts in various fields were seconded to the departments as advisers to ministers. I became acquainted with a Cambridge economist who was brought in to advise ministers. He won his spurs on occasions when he could give non-obvious advice that mandarins who had studied classics at Oxford would not suggest. But he was ignored much of the time.

Reform of the civil service seemed to creep along in the wake of the report. Two decades later, Prime Minister Margaret Thatcher moved the civil service in the directions suggested by Fulton, illustrating the gradual nature of reform in England. Some of Wilson's ministers, particularly Anthony Crosland in his book *The Future of Socialism*, anticipated what would later become "the third way" for Prime Minister Tony Blair after 1997, a way that closely resembled Bill Clinton's New Democrat ideas.

One of my best feature stories was a series of interviews with young professionals who were easily spotted as innovative in their fields. They were promising young politicians, academic experts serving in government temporarily, and activists in legal reform, fifty in all. They divided roughly into Left, Center, and Right; however, they were not traditionalists, and ideology and occupation did not coincide. Those on the Left echoed the ideas of Crosland and the Labour government. Some were active in race relations, the abolition of capital punishment, and "third way" politics and economics. The Tories sounded like Thatcherites ahead of their time, and two of them became ministers in Thatcher's cabinet. They were strong for capitalist values in English life and hostile to the dead weight of traditional institutions. People in the centrist group, which seemed to adhere loosely to the Liberal Party, were much like American Democrats, part of a messy middle but seemingly closer to Labour reformers, for they rejected traditional socialism. They all adhered to the virtues of English gradualism, with a respect for tradition while they deplored stale tradition. They did not want Britain to become the hard-thrusting society of America. The old and the new had to be joined in ways to be worked out in practice.

My conclusion from my stories was that the United Kingdom was on the verge of institutional reforms responsive to markets, efficiency, and productivity. Yet it took twenty years for Margaret Thatcher to appear and dramatically demand of her potential new ministers, "Is he one of us?" Tony Blair then returned to Crosland's ideas for his third way in 1997. I had spotted the trends, however, and later wrote stories about how England had changed. A separate chapter had yet to be written then as Tony Blair left the government and Labour governments lost their fire about what had actually been achieved.

Those five years at the England bureau were the most enjoyable I have ever had. Then Buck Dorsey returned like Zeus in 1970 and announced that I was going to the Washington bureau to cover economic policy. When I hesitated, saying that I was not an economist, he paid no attention. I had covered English economic policy, hadn't I?

We wanted to stay in England forever. We had had wonderful holidays in Cornwell, Devon, Yorkshire, Scotland, and Wales, plus short and long trips to France and points east. On my last day at work, I was eating a sandwich and lamenting our imminent departure while I was sitting on a bench in St. James Park. Molly had reestablished her career by writing about England for American audiences. I could find a job but at much less pay. I had a good career waiting for me at home, and we wanted Alice to grow up as an American. We loved London, but it was time to go. We resolved to return often.

We bought a house in Chevy Chase, and I began to learn the ropes from my predecessor, Charlie Davis, who was retiring. We went to the Treasury, the Federal Reserve, and the White House to meet the men in charge as well as other economic staffers. It was a cohesive community in that they were bounded by the debates among economists about the greater or lesser place for the intervention of government in the economy. Next, we attacked the Hill and chairmen and ranking minority leaders of the key committees. Again, we found much agreement aside from their partisan rhetoric.

Then I spent considerable time and shoe leather trying to find sources who would tell me something if I asked for information. I had to persuade them that I would respect their privacy and get the story straight, or they wouldn't talk again. I could not be partisan and had to present events in a fair way. I also found friends in other departments that dealt with economic policies, and I cultivated a number of economists whom I found sensible. My bureau colleagues also helped as stories overlapped. Our stories were written for a public beyond Baltimore, for we were seen as a national paper.

My first big story came in the summer of 1971, when Nixon tried to freeze inflation through wage and price controls. He was not about to tighten money through fiscal policy; he believed that he had lost in 1960 because tight money had continued the recession. The problem of rising inflation was built into management-labor contracts, which boosted prices and wages year after year with the implicit confidence that the federal government would not let the balloon burst, because that would mean high unemployment. So Nixon froze everything. His economists were against the move, but they were not running for office.

Economists told me that Nixon's eyes glazed over in economic discussions, but he knew about politics. The president would send plays to George Allen the coach of the Washington Redskins. He believed in dramatic action and not what he called Ohio State football, "three yards and a cloud of dust." I got a tip on the economic story early from a friend in the British Embassy who told me that the U.K. government had secretly asked Washington to back up the pound for a limited period. In response, Nixon considered freezing gold for that purpose and imposing wage and

price controls for ninety days. The policy was developed by a small group
of advisers at Camp David in August. Nixon was much influenced by the
tough Texan John Connally, who was secretary of the treasury and was
trying to protect the president politically. Herbert Stein, one of Nixon's
economic advisers, later said that "the clamor was for a non-fattening hot
fudge sundae."

I was prepared to write a full story because of all the interviews I
had done. That was the mark of a good reporter—being prepared—but
I reverted to daily and bread-and-butter work during the next year when
wage and price controls were lifted and then reimposed. Stein, by then the
head of the CEA, told the president that controls could not be reimposed
because "you can never step in the same river twice."

Nixon responded, "You can if it's frozen."

Stein then gave up.

Molly and I loved our life in Washington. Alice went to school, and
we visited the wonderful zoo, went to the Delaware beaches, and took
trips home to North Carolina, the home of Alice's grandparents, and the
lake. We often saw John and George. I was forty-two years old in 1972,
and life was good.

CHAPTER 8

John
Success, Uncertainty, and
Affirmation, 1960–1985

I moved into a small apartment in Manhattan near New York Hospital in 1960. I was thirty years old, and my academic career had begun. In my position as assistant professor at the hospital, I taught and saw patients in the large outpatient clinic and hospital.

George, Clay, and I met briefly at home in the summer, and while we were all on our way, we were lonely and hoping to get married. The problem was that none of us had any prospects. We were all working too hard to pursue girls for the sheer fun of the chase, and we were tired of dating.

In the autumn of 1960, my aunt and uncle invited me to a cocktail party. They wanted to introduce me to their friends, but I figured that would be pretty dull. They threw in some eligible girls, though, and I had not been there long when I noticed a good-looking girl with auburn hair on the far side of the room. I worked my way toward her. As she finished a conversation, I blundered right in and said, "I'm John McDonald. We have not met, but I would like to meet you."

She smiled and replied in a wonderful southern accent, "I'm Sally Bell, and now we have met."

I felt at ease immediately. "I'm from North Carolina. Have I kept my accent?"

"Oh, yes. But how do you know we aren't related? All southerners are related."

"Just kissin' cousins is fine."

Then we got into it. She was from Richmond and had been living in New York for two years, working in an art gallery. Her uncle, who was a law partner of my uncle, had helped her get the job. Of course, we had mutual friends. She had been to Sweet Briar and had known boys from Yale.

"I'm a psychiatrist at Cornell and have just come to town," I explained to her.

"I don't know anything about psychiatry," she said. "In Richmond, we just put auntie in the closet and shut the door."

This easy conversation went back and forth all night as I took her to eat at my favorite Italian restaurant. I liked her so much because she was not standoffish like Mary and Rachel. We shared such an implicit cultural bond that we would almost finish each other's sentences.

One thing led to another, and I eventually went to Richmond to meet her parents that winter. They asked me about "my people," and they were satisfied with the long line of planters, Presbyterian ministers, doctors, and lawyers I could summon up. Her "people" were much the same, too. I was now an Episcopalian, which was fine as well.

My father came to New York to meet her and was entranced. Of course, I took her home before the wedding. She thought the town was charming but a bit "country." We were married in St. Catherine's Church in Richmond, and we had a large wedding party that included George, John, Clay, and Charlie from Fort Worth.

Sally had a trust fund of her own, which helped us buy a brownstone on the east side of Manhattan, and we settled in quickly. I began to make some money, and we were able to afford to have three children and send them to private schools. I became an associate professor at Cornell in due course, and Sally joined the Junior League and volunteered in countless ways.

I had had two years of psychoanalysis, the last year having been limited in scope. I would need further supervised training to become an analyst, but I did not want to just listen to people lying on a couch. I enjoyed the back and forth of therapy too much. New drugs were coming along that could be combined with therapy in good ways as well, but analysts usually avoided drugs.

Most psychoanalysts in New York at that time were orthodox Freudians bound rigidly to Freud's dictums, which I found too constraining. My early interest was in building bridges between pharmacology in psychiatry and the dynamic clinical psychology of psychotherapy. Clinical psychologists were trained to work with patients, because they studied personality systematically, whereas we were trained in an ad hoc case method in hospitals, with some personality theory added. Our objective was not to understand personality but to cure individuals as best we could.

After I had gotten my feet on the ground, I recommended to my department chairman that he hire a few clinical psychologists to work with residents to broaden our capabilities. He eventually agreed and put me in charge of a new program in education and treatment that included psychiatrists and psychologists. I began to reflect on what my analysis had taught me about my need to build bridges, this having originated in my own divided family. The energy for my work came from these early conflicts, and in the search for resolution, I was able to create fresh approaches.

Family life was happy in the sixties. We had John in 1962, Sarah in 1964, and Amy in 1966. They enjoyed a happy, sophisticated life in Manhattan, going to museums, the theater, opera, and so on, often accompanied by lots of friends with sophisticated parents. We went to Gibson Island off the coast of Maryland every summer, where Sally's parents often went, and I reconnected with some of my friends from Hopkins who were still in Baltimore.

In 1970, I was forty, and Sally was thirty-five. I was working very hard and did not realize that my work was swallowing me up until it was too late. Only the children held us together, and they complained when I missed school plays or competitive games. I plunged into everything: teaching medical students, working with residents and young faculty members, treating patients, raising money, running research groups, and hammering it all into articles with my coworkers. Through it all, I was making a name for myself. I took a secondary position in the department of medicine to work with patients suffering from psychosomatic illnesses. I traveled a lot to lecture and found it wearing but exhilarating.

Sally was so busy that she didn't seem to me to notice anything about my work and its effect on her. My work was both forbidding and uninteresting to her anyway, and she was uncomfortable when my colleagues talked about their cases at parties. Sally barely tolerated my friends, whether physicians, writers, or scholars, and her friends were the wives of lawyers and businessmen. Our dinner parties were either one-sided or discordant, depending on the guests.

I had enjoyed Sally's soft southern touch in life but had forgotten that the soft touch may have a steel edge to it. Southern women often like to control things, even as they seem to give in. We were going in different directions, but my skills as a therapist were of no help to avoid this. I enjoyed my family but did not study it.

We fell into a summer routine. Sally and the children would go to Gibson Island for July and August, and I would go for two or three weeks in the middle of summer. It was lonely in New York, but I wanted the kids to enjoy the island as much as they could. It was a common pattern among professional and well-to-do families for the children and their mothers to be away from town during the summers.

We went to my home every other year for a few days, and the grandparents came to New York. George, Clay, and I arranged for overlap at home, but Sally and Peggy could not get along. Everyone loved Molly. Peggy pushed Sally about politics, and of course, none of us, especially Sally, was radical enough for her. Sally refused to talk, and George was embarrassed by Peggy. Sally thought the lake was a dump compared to Gibson Island, and so did Peggy, who wanted to get back to work in Providence.

On Sally's island, I felt out of place with all the posh people among whom she was at home. I admit that I was a snob about uninteresting businessmen and lawyers and their "dumb" wives, and I found Sally's parent's friends almost more than I could stand. They were all for the Vietnam War and hated the Great Society. I just kept my mouth shut and tried not to rise to the bait.

When Sally and the children returned home for school in September 1975, I sensed that something was wrong. She asked that we go out to dinner, because she wanted to talk. We went to the same Italian restaurant where I had once courted her, and as soon as we ordered drinks, she said, looking me square in the eye, "I'm not happy."

"I see that you're restless. What's the problem?" I asked.

"I felt so at home on the island, being with people I have known forever and are like family to me."

"Do you miss Richmond?"

"Oh, yes, I do," she said. "I've been happy in New York, but it is so big and so lonely so much of the time. We have acquaintances, but I long for really close friends like the ones at home."

"Tell me more."

"You love the excitement that your ambition creates, but that's not for me."

"What do you want to do? I could move to Hopkins or Duke."

There was a long pause. She looked flustered. Then she said, "I met someone at the island this summer, someone from the past. Do you remember Charlie Best?"

Charlie had been an old boyfriend of hers who had married another girl before we had gotten married. His wife had died of cancer two years ago.

"We saw a lot of Charlie this summer. He and Daddy play golf together, and I know his sister Mary well." She then added this unkind cut: "He took the children sailing, and they just loved it."

I did not say anything, but as a therapist, I let her carry on. She was no longer flustered and had hit her stride. "He has two motherless children," she then said. "They are living with his mother."

I still didn't say anything.

"I'm confused. I miss home so much," she continued. "Maybe I should try living there for a while to find out who I really am. The children will go to good schools. I would get to know Charlie better. Your life is so full here. You will do fine. I don't feel part of your life here."

I understood her words. They were authentic Sally. I then realized how much we had lived in separate worlds, some of which was my fault. But deep down the truth was that we were not well matched. I had loved her southern ways but had outgrown my own while I had taken her into an alien land.

"I don't want to stand in your way," I told her. "Make your plans."

"Oh, John, I'm so sorry."

She was sorry, but I could see the anticipation in her eyes for a clean break and a new life. The children were told that the separation was temporary and that Daddy might move to a medical school near Richmond soon. Off they went.

I never doubted that the marriage was over, and I knew that I would miss the children more than Sally. She had been my ornament of southern charm in New York. The house was lonely after they left. I could not cook and had no interest in eating alone, so I ate out at night, most often at the Yale Club. My friends were wonderful for a while, but life soon returned to normal from their perspective.

I began to consider getting therapy from a good psychiatrist. Then my priest at the Church of the Epiphany suggested that I meet with a pastoral counselor at the church who was both a priest and a clinical psychologist, and I agreed to do it. Like many Episcopal priests, my counselor, Geoffrey Hunt, was very interested in Carl Jung, the psychologist. Jung's writing paid special attention to the second half of life when one asked questions about the meaning of one's life in the present and in the future and reached for spiritual as well as psychological answers. Freud once said that he "stayed in the basement," but Jung reached higher. Jungians believed that the failure to ask existential questions about one's life could be harmful to one, perhaps causing a failure to grow and adapt to the next challenges of life.

Geoffrey was about my age, and he was very relaxed and friendly. I was grieving for myself more than for Sally, but I felt that I had created a great failure in my life. We got to my mother's death pretty quickly. I did not blame myself for her death, but her absence had given me an unconscious sense of fragility that Sally had filled. I was a work engine with a fear of intimacy. Sally was perfect on the surface, but we had never bonded. It was not all my fault. She did not like my way of life or my ambition.

When I wrote Sally a long letter about all this, she seemed to understand what I was talking about. She was enjoying the life she loved. The children, who were now thirteen, eleven, and nine, came to New York for Christmas, and I could see that they had handled the move easily. They missed me, and I had to fend off questions about my plans. Then they were gone. Sally eventually told me that she wanted a divorce so that she could marry Charlie. I would have to share only the children's school and college tuition payments with her. She had plenty of money.

Geoffrey and I began to explore whether I was still suffering from my mother's death in my anxiety and loneliness or some existential issues that might have been plaguing me. I was a good nominal Episcopalian with all the standard beliefs but without a spiritual life. My Presbyterian origins had given me a powerful work ethic, and that was how I understood religion. What else was there? I had often felt that something was there, and that was why I had been drawn to the Anglican way; however, it was so easy to be a happy Episcopalian without any depth, and besides, I had relaxed in my ways. Now I began to search the unknown.

At Geoffrey's suggestion, I became a consultant to several pastoral counseling centers at Episcopal churches. Pastoral counselors were generally priests or ministers with training in clinical psychology who helped people deal with personal problems. They were trained to give therapy and bring in the perspective of faith if clients were receptive. This work grew on me, and I began to feel a new spirit within me that I could not name. It had not visited me during secular therapy. I kept my standard psychiatric work quite separate from this new work.

Although I was not with them very often, I had kept in close touch with the children, John especially, and in 1980 he entered Yale. His mother favored the University of Virginia, but the young man knew his own mind. It was a coming together that I almost could not believe. We saw a lot of each other in the next years, visiting each other in New Haven and New York. I got to know his friends and loved my immersion back into Yale life. It was a different and more interesting place for me, because the students were of a much greater variety and the education offered so much more than it had in my years. John decided that he wanted to become an actor, and I saw him in a number of plays at the Yale Dramat. I thought that he was excellent. He had his mother's looks and her ability to charm an audience. The two girls went to Sweet Briar, which was fine with me. That was what their mother wanted, anyway.

Meanwhile, I had to adapt to a changing psychiatry. A muted conflict began to emerge in medical schools and hospitals between psychoanalysis and psychotherapy, on the one hand, and pharmacological psychiatry, on the other. Psychiatrists took sides but the trends clearly favored the latter. New tranquilizers and antidepressants came on the market, and drug companies pushed them hard to doctors. A new generation of psychiatrists preferred drugs over therapy, particularly for psychotic patients, and there was merit in some of their claims. Medical schools and hospitals also put pressure on psychiatrists to adopt the "medical model" of treatment in psychiatry in which the physician identified the illness and prescribed the remedy with medication, without knowing much about the patient as an individual. All that talking and getting to know the patient as an individual cost too much time and money. The old prejudice that talking therapy was not medicine seemed to be verified. No one asked whether or not the new drugs were any good, but to be fair, some of them were. Medical students preferred pills to talk, because they could easily study the illness and apply a tangible, quick remedy. They needed only to find the cause and cure it. I thought that the process would surely fall out of favor, because they were now treating people with emotional problems with drugs that might not have been sufficient. Therapy might have been needed as well.

The heads of departments were increasingly pharmacologists rather than psychoanalysts, which was all right if they were tolerant of many paths to wellness, but that was not always the case. I wrote a few papers and then a short book on these questions, arguing for balanced approaches.

It received some favorable attention from psychologists, theologians, and public intellectuals, but the medical establishment was hard to penetrate.

I thought of going into private practice full-time, but that would have been a retreat from the very issues of academic medicine that bothered me. On the spur of the moment, I decided to study psychology and religion at Union Theological Seminary up the island in Manhattan. I wanted a new adventure, and this seemed the best path. I trimmed my practice back a bit and registered for courses that interested me.

The work consisted of analyzing different psychotherapies for their implicit understanding of human nature. Freud stayed in the basement, and Jung was quasi-mystical. Humanistic psychologists like Carl Rogers were optimistic about reasonable self-understanding and ignored the perversity and stubbornness of human nature. I found myself closest to the ego psychologists like Heinz Hartmann, who saw us as creatures with a reasoning ego in the midst of unconscious, moral, and cultural forces that could overwhelm us and needed unpacking through therapy. In my mind, this conception of human nature was closest to a Jewish and Christian idea of human nature as good but flawed. The ideas of self-understanding, confession, repentance, forgiveness, and health seemed to me to match my views of ego psychology, which was practiced by psychiatrists trying to broaden Freud.

I wondered if religious faith might have been a resource for psychological therapy, because it brought a greater sense of human fragility and the resources of faith to the task of curing ills. Secular therapy was fine, but perhaps the existential problems of life about identity, purpose, and finality might have been resolved by understanding one's life as part of a larger spiritual story and destiny. Secular therapy did not address such questions. Faith and therapy were matched in the uncertain, ragged course that each took, but always with hope.

If my patients were receptive to faith, we would talk about it and take a few steps in that direction. I found that they might grow in ways that would complement their therapy. I also found that strengthening the ego through therapy could enhance faith. For example, a Buddhist patient from Thailand was far too passive in the face of an authoritarian uncle who led the family import-export business. My patient was deeply into meditation and self-effacement as a good Buddhist, but his ego needed to be strengthened in order to stand up to his uncle, which he eventually did. His two sides were more united as a result.

Most of my colleagues in academic psychiatry would not even listen to such ideas. However, psychiatrists and clinical psychologists in private practice responded to my writing and talks about these things, because they genuinely wanted to help people. They knew how weak psychiatric theory was, and they were selective in their practices, so anything that helped was accepted.

At age fifty-five, I knew that I had been working too hard and had been lonely for some time, even though my son, John, had finished Yale Drama School and was living with me and acting part-time. I was too old to date a lot and never liked the blind dates that my friends arranged for me. One night after work, I decided that I did not want to cook and eat alone—John was in a play—so I went over to the Yale Club to eat.

Just as I entered the dining room, I saw an old friend named Jack Dawkins, an internist, and his wife sitting with a lovely woman with dark black hair. I was invited to join them and was introduced to Julie Adams, an old friend and clinical psychologist from Chicago who had come to town for a meeting. She had a mischievous look in her green eyes as if she was inviting me to join an adventure. She knew my work and actually liked it.

Julie and I began to talk back and forth as if Jack and his wife had disappeared. The talk broadened during dinner, and I was thinking how I could see more of Julie, not later but now. She had been married to a Chicago lawyer who had been killed in a plane accident some years ago. She had not remarried and had studied and eventually practiced psychotherapy.

In desperation, I invited all of them back to my brownstone. Julie clearly wanted to come, and the Dawkins were not going to object, because she was staying with them, so off we went. Soon enough, young John came home, and I invited him to join us. Like many actors, he was shy, but he brightened up when Julie asked him about his play, Harold Pinter's *The Homecoming*. The play was about a power struggle between the father of a family of sons and the wife of one of them. It was only resolved at the end in an ambiguous way. John had played the husband of the wily wife, who always got her way.

The rest of us listened as they explored Pinter and his ambiguities. Julie said that she sometimes brought stories from literature into therapy and gave us some illustrations. I was afraid that I was going to lose her to my son, but she accepted my invitation to lunch the next day. We never looked back. We were married three months later, and she set up practice at Cornell. It was magical.

CHAPTER 9

George
Retreat, 1975–1983

After our divorce, Peggy and I saw little of each other at Brown. She was happy with women's studies, and her scholarship blossomed. I entered a dry period during which I wrote a few essays about the "new Right" in American politics with special attention to the neo-conservatives who founded and wrote in *The Public Interest* about the failings of the Great Society and the weak American posture toward the Soviet Union. A number of these people had been Trotskyites in their youth, then anti-Stalinists, and now fierce anti-Communists. They saw themselves as realists in contrast to Democrats of the Left who, they thought, trusted far too much in the efficacy of government. Such writers became the intellectual foundation of the ideas that lay behind the creation of the Heritage Foundation, the American Enterprise Institute, and waves of new ideas in law schools, economic thought, and new journals. I could not join them, because despite my skepticism of liberal thought and programs, I could not abandon progressive goals in favor of "devil take the hindmost" individualism of the new Right. It seemed to me that their ideology paralyzed their practicality so that their politics would be primarily rhetorical.

I was getting tired of this hobby horse, however, and snapped up an invitation to teach at the University of Virginia for the 1981–2 academic year. I could do whatever I wanted but was invited to participate in a series of oral history interviews with former members of the Carter White House. The interviews were conducted by the staff and guests of a research center on the presidency. It was an effort to capture the fresh memories of Carter people before those memories hardened into certainties.

Clay, who had covered the Carter presidency, joined a few of the sessions, and our approaches blended. He knew the Carter people well and, along with others, could probe into events with skill. My preference was to explore how the White House worked under Jimmy Carter particularly in response to Carter's own personality.

The interviews lasted a day and a half, including shared meals, so one got a pretty good idea of the Carter people, individually and collectively. They brought two general ideas to the table. First, Jimmy Carter's presidency had somehow failed. Second, Carter's attempt to take Democrats back to the political center was sound, and Great Society politics and policy were no longer fruitful. There had to be a neoliberal adaptation. Many, if not most, congressional Democrats did not want to hear that, and Carter was a lonely prophet in his own party.

Ronald Reagan then stole Carter's thunder with a more radical message but with the same themes. Carter had tried to create a balance across the two liberal centers, and he had failed. I later saw Bill Clinton and Tony Blair more clearly as a result of these disclosures about Carter, and it all helped me later fill out my understanding of the strengths and weaknesses of contemporary liberalism.

Brown wanted to know if I would return in 1982, but I was sitting with a Virginia offer in hand and politely said no. My decision to stay at Virginia was perhaps a piece of my uncertainties about liberalism. I did not want to go back into the hyperliberal atmosphere at Brown, which was highly intolerant, and even though I was not a conservative, I wanted freedom to breathe. My history colleagues at Brown had been wonderful, but there were good colleagues at Virginia, too. I also wanted to get away from Peggy. I did, however, see quite a bit of Clay and Molly, who were now in Washington. Molly had become a mother-confessor to John and me about our failed marriages. John and I asked ourselves what our marriages had lacked that Clay and Molly's had created. John thought that the happiness of Clay's parents was important. He had grown up in a happy family. But how did he have the good sense to pick Molly? We could not answer that, but Clay did admit his own marvelous mother had taught him something by example. We knew that John's stepmother had failed on that score. My mother was wonderful in her own way, but she was an exotic spirit, a southern flower, unique to herself. Neither of us had gained much to guide us in picking girls to marry.

I was happy in my work at UVA, but my personal life was in the dumps. I had never had a happy relationship with a woman my own age, and here I was past forty. I had no children and not much family. My father was dead, and my mother had moved back to Mobile. My two sisters, with whom I had never been close, were leading society lives in Nashville and Charlotte, two New South cities that were booming. Their husbands were nice fellows with whom I could talk for a few minutes, but they had no comprehension of my work or life. We had the occasional holiday together.

In short, I was lonely and unfulfilled. I had never been a very good Presbyterian and had shed any patina of faith, although my temperament made it impossible for me to be a militant atheist or even an agnostic. I was in limbo. So, as I wallowed in a vacuum, I decided that I needed a fresh project: it was time to write another book. I had done all I that wanted to do with FDR and the New Deal. My portraits of liberalism and its enemies were fine, but I had to wait on the politics of the next few years. Reagan was sitting smugly in the White House and doing much better than I had thought he would. He understood something about how to be president that Carter had never understood, but I was not a journalist. What to do? My interest in Franklin Roosevelt had been in large part a curiosity about how a master politician did his work. But the great master was an enigma to me and probably to everyone else, because he wore his mask so well. One could see his strategies of persuasion and manipulation from the outside, but the inner man was invisible. I had done enough to set out FDR's style and skill. I settled on writing essays on Theodore Roosevelt, which might have added up to a book. I did not want to undertake a full biography, but individual essays seemed manageable. Then, one day, chance took over my life.

I saw a sign advertising a lecture on "Shakespeare's English Kings." That interested me, so I went in and sat down. The talk was to be given by Professor Anne English, whom I did not know. She was a good-looking brunette with a lovely, melodious voice, and she spoke very well. Her talk was about the English history plays of the great master: *Richard II; Henry IV, Parts 1 and 2; Henry V; Henry VI;* and *Richard III.* Her analysis was primarily literary, but I could see implicit themes that she did not fully develop about the dangers of seizing power by force and the difficulty of establishing legitimacy and authority after such a seizure. Was Shakespeare defending traditional medieval monarchy, or was he describing a series of human dilemmas? Henry V had seemed to reestablish legitimacy for his authority; however, his son, Henry VI had lost that authority, and Richard III had abused authority, eventually overthrown by Henry VII. But the Tudors were not medieval kings. Was Shakespeare writing for the Tudor monarchs?

After the talk, I went up to Professor English and raised these questions with her. She stressed the crucial point that there was no final or orthodox interpretation of any of the plays. Shakespeare created ambiguity and uncertainty that permitted different interpretations and gave leeway for directors and stage productions. The conversation led to lunch, and we became friends. I was drawn to this historical drama, because one could see it in the life of Teddy Roosevelt. He always pressed himself to the limit, testing his physical strength and skill but also launching one political adventure after another, driven by the wish for policy achievement and also by a personality that needed to win over others in order to quiet private fears. As president, he was a brilliant politician who played the art of the possible beautifully and preached to the nation about the virtues of reform. He showed great self-restraint when in office, much along the lines of my advocacy of prudent, incremental leadership. But once he was out of office, his desire to return to the White House overwhelmed him, and he challenged his chosen successor, William Howard Taft. Thus, he made Woodrow Wilson president in 1912. It was a morality tale of sorts. If TR had been able to wait until 1916, he might have won the Republican nomination and the presidency again, but he could not wait. The comparison with Anne's English kings was not exact, except to the extent that it illustrated the dangers of politicians who sought the power to govern not only because they want to achieve things but also because they need it desperately for the fulfillment of their own personalities.

Anne and I began to talk about looking even more fully at her kings as political personalities and perhaps add some Roman plays to broaden the drama. She had published several articles on the history plays and was open to the idea of collaborating in an essay that examined kings as politicians. A central question would be this: Did Shakespeare have a thesis about moral leadership? Richard II was a weak man who acted in arbitrary ways and yet complained that his opponents did not understand that he was the king by birth and divine right. God would not permit his overthrow. Lord Bolingbroke, who removed him from the throne, could have asserted his rights to the title and property that Richard had snatched away from his father and left the king in place, but he deposed Richard in an artful way by having him renounce the throne. But this did not confer his legitimacy, because civil war had broken out between Henry and the very nobles who supported his ambitions. Shakespeare's portrait of Henry IV had been one of ambition that had exceeded its reach, and he lamented his inability to unite the nation. His son, Prince Hal, became Henry V and hoped to unite the nation in a war against France. Henry was depicted as a warrior king of heroic mold, and yet he manipulated English bishops to support his claim, threatened to destroy the town of Harfleur if it did not surrender, ordered the killing of French prisoners as the tide of battle shifted, and inspired his soldiers with his rhetoric about England. It was essentially a war about his claims to land. He died before his time, and his weak son, Henry VI, lost the crown to the house of York. The Duke of York, Richard III, was a murderer and a tyrant defeated by Henry Tudor, who assumed the throne as Henry VII and the founder of the Tudor dynasty.

One could maintain that Shakespeare had written a long epic in praise of the Tudors. Henry V was thus made a national hero, as celebrated by Lawrence Olivier in the 1944 movie, a beautiful propaganda film made to support the Allies' war effort. Or one could argue that Henry was a hero king or his father's son, a Machiavelli in heroic disguise.

But what did Shakespeare think of him? We do not know. Perhaps he was saying that a nation required such strong, effective leadership, especially when one saw the anarchy that came with Henry VI. The anarchy gave rise to villainy during the reign of Richard III, which led to its own destruction. It seems that Shakespeare could not find a genuine moral leader.

He explored the same question in *Julius Caesar*. Brutus, a good republican and a good man, was manipulated by Cassius, a jealous intriguer, to participate in Caesar's murder, for fear of dictatorship. Mark Antony and Octavius Caesar filled the vacuum and created an authoritarian regime to succeed the republic. Shakespeare did not give us a morally good ruler. In his last play, *The Tempest*, Prospero, who had lost his dukedom to his brother because of his own failings as a king, gave up his magical powers and returned home to take on the burdens of politics at which he failed before.

Anne contributed an analysis of the plays and the competing interpretations, and in answer to the question about whether Shakespeare had a conception of moral leadership or not, I concluded that he knew what he would like to see in a moral leader but did not create examples in the plays. Shakespeare was not amoral. No, he was a realist who portrayed political life as he found it.

Our essay was well received, but our fields were too different for continued collaboration. She had more to do on Shakespeare, and I was still having fun with TR. We began to live together. She met John and Clay and their wives, and in good time, we married. I was deeply happy for the first time in my life. I continued to write, enjoyed teaching more than ever, and settled down to a quiet life.

There was one new element. Anne was a Quaker. I went to Quaker meetings with her even though my religious feelings were somewhat vague. I found that I enjoyed the quiet interspersed by a few remarks, usually thoughtful ones. It was spiritually restful. I felt in tune with something but did not try to articulate it. My life with Anne reinforced the spirit. I had finally come home.

CHAPTER 10

Clay
The Great Disappointment, 1986–1996

Newspapers had always been a business, but at least with some family-owned papers, the purpose was to produce a good paper with enough profits to survive at a high level of quality. Doing this became harder and harder for papers in St. Louis, Louisville, and Milwaukee, especially for the *New York Herald Tribune* and other good papers, including the *Sun*. Families lost interest or fell out among themselves, or the paper just could not make it. Younger members of the two families that had owned and sustained the *Sun* for many years finally sold it for a profit to the Los Angeles Times Mirror Company in 1986. Circulation was declining. There was competition from a new, free daily paper. The newsroom was shrinking in size. In 2000, the Times Mirror Company was purchased by the Tribune Company of Chicago, but I had already left in 1987. The economic hard times continued with staff and budget cuts. I had been the head of the Washington bureau for three years, and after the sale, we had lost two out of eight staffers, and two of the six foreign bureaus had been subsequently eliminated. Talented people began to leave the paper because the good jobs were drying up.

My situation with the paper seemed to be all right. My essays for the *New Yorker* and the *Times* Sunday magazine helped pay the bills over and above my salary, and I became known as a good popular writer on economic policy. This strengthened my position at the paper somewhat, but new editors were brought in as veterans were summarily fired. I decided to leave if I could, but it was not easy to find another job at age fifty-seven.

Then one day, I received a call from a friend in the *New York Times* Washington bureau. The head of the bureau, Harry Adams, was going back home to North Carolina to resume the editorship of a very fine paper in a medium-sized city. He had been editor before he had gone to Washington and wanted a new managing editor. He was about sixty, and I had known him for years. The new publisher of the paper, Frank Smith, also a North Carolinian, was leaving Louisville for a last job. Southerners wanting to go home was not unusual. It was sometimes called the "back to Egypt" feeling.

I let Adams know that I was interested, but I wanted to explore the possibility, both the job and a feeling of nostalgia and familiarity about home. In due course, Molly and I went down to see about it, and we liked everything we saw. I was tired of covering a beat, even though I enjoyed managing the bureau. Of course, this was a bigger job. I would oversee the news divisions and act as part of the three-person management team. Nothing was mentioned explicitly about my succeeding Harry as editor, but the implications were clear.

The paper had been owned by the Ravenal family for fifty years. A Ravenal was usually publisher and chairman of the board, but the present senior Ravenal, Guy, was president of the largest local bank. He bore the title of president of the paper but worked closely with the editorial staff in supportive ways and left its management to the publisher and the editor.

Molly and I turned the idea over and over and considered it from every angle. Primarily as onlookers, we had seen a lot of the big-time world in London and Washington. One eventually realized that national leaders were not that different from the rest of us. They were just more pretentious; only a relative few were greatly talented. It was fun to be close to power or the appearance of power, but plenty of people did that. Most importantly, I wanted to go home. George had found a home in Charlottesville. John had to remain in New York because of his work, but George and I knew that even though John had done his best to carve out his own sphere, he was tired of fighting battles in large medical organizations. Each of us was trying to find a "small platoon" on a human scale.

I eventually accepted the job, and we moved. Harry Adams and Frank Smith were veteran newsmen. The news staff was a combination of seasoned reporters who knew North Carolina and the region well and smart young men and women who fully expected to work up and out of the paper. The paper had sent a number of good reporters to our one-person Washington bureau over the years, and it was known as a good place to start a career. We could have engaged in routine coverage of local events and institutions at a mediocre level and been taken for granted by the readers, but that was not what the owners or the staff wanted. They wanted a jewel that would be the very best in its class. That meant searching out stories and writing them well while we preserved news and editorial independence.

Simultaneous pressures for quality had to come from below and above, joined by a shared pride in the result.

I began by getting acquainted with the editors—state, city, business, sports, and so forth—and then meeting government officials, leading politicians, business nabobs, and civic leaders. Gradually, I put together my own sociological map of the city and the region. The changes since my boyhood were remarkable. For the most part, people were better educated and certainly better off economically, and provincial "southernness" was far less obvious. There was still a dark side to North Carolina politics. The state had been led by fairly progressive politicians, especially among governors and senators, but Jesse Helms had played upon deep rural and small-town resentments against the elites of the state. Helms stirred up anger about all the changes that had improved the lives of many but also left large swatches of the rural and the uneducated behind. It was a very uneven economy and political culture. The paper was at odds with this culture and had to be careful not to trigger eruptions from below. My job was to nurture a high quality of reporting and keep a balance among the stories so that we were a good local newspaper and yet carried sufficient national news and analysis. We could not be the *Baltimore Sun*, but we did not want to be the local "shopper," either.

Coverage of race was particularly tricky. School integration was a continual question usually as a result of court decisions about busing or school closings, white flight, and the quality of increasingly all-black schools. We tried to play it straight as reporters. The few editorial writers pretty much stayed with the spirit of Supreme Court decisions. They were for integration but not so sure about busing white and black students back and forth if it led to white flight into private schools. We took flack from progressive whites and blacks, and white conservatives were on us all the time for being too "liberal." We tried to find a center position but were never sure if we had many followers. We knew we were going where the nation would go, but it was going to be painful everywhere. Eventually, we supported the idea of good neighborhood schools, whether white or black, without busing, but again, it was tricky, although the idea came from black leaders.

We were able to write stories critical of local industries, because the owners also owned the bank. This was a tethered idealism. For example, a college-age son of one of our editors worked in a large bag company for the summer along with a number of minimum-wage blacks, and he was appalled at the working conditions. Dust was very heavy in the air.

Ventilation was poor, and the risks for lung disease seemed great. He told his father, who asked me to look into it. We did not write a story immediately but sent a tip to the state department of health to investigate the situation. Then we wrote about the investigation. The family that owned the factory knew our role, but it did them no good to complain about the paper to its owners in light of the department of health's negative findings. Instead of crusading, we used the subtle influence of the paper, which could sometimes backfire, too.

The partisan stance of the paper and its editorial page had long been a moderate Democratic tone. This stance could be easily maintained as long as North Carolina sent Democrats to congress in large numbers and had periodic Democratic governors. The Republicans statewide were Eisenhower people who began to move into the Reagan camp on taxes, budgets, and national defense. The continuance of healthy partisan debate in state politics permitted us to present our views in a moderate spirit without the broadsides from conservative Republicans that came later as the Republicans became a predominantly conservative southern party. In any event, the paper was making money and winning national journalism awards.

When Guy Ravenal, the patriarch of the family, president of the bank and the paper, died at the age of eighty-five in 1995, his son, Owen, succeeded to the presidency of the bank. Owen was less interested in the paper than his father had been, but he fully expected to become the paper's president. The position seemed set until he was challenged by his brother-in-law, the husband of Owen's sister, Betty, who was a lawyer in Charlotte. Ed Davis had always been interested in the paper and had sat on the board and represented his wife's shares, but no one expected the challenge. Stock was divided among the widow, Dorothy, a lovely woman who cared little for business; two other daughters, Sarah and Eugenia; and Ed and Betty. No one individual owned a majority of stock after the senior Ravenal's death. The family attorney, who was also the lawyer for the paper, found himself in a conflict of interest between his two clients and withdrew altogether, so several lawyers joined the fray.

Betty had always resented her older brother's position as heir for personal reasons that went back a long time, and she stood behind her husband's ambitions. Her two sisters sided with her. Their two husbands stayed out of it, and they all had the same lawyer who had been brought in from Charlotte. Owen had support from his mother. A count of the stock gave him a slight edge and therefore made him the winner, but it would be a hollow victory, because it was now clear that turmoil in the board would hamper the professional leadership of the paper.

Adams and Smith were nervous, both for themselves and for the paper. They did not try to mediate for fear they would be drawn into the fray, and the various lawyers were antagonistic now that lines had been drawn. Dorothy Ravenal loved all her children, even though she opposed her daughter's actions; however, she was not the person to mediate. She could only plead for all to be reasonable. Ed Davis was the main cause of the trouble, for he played on his wife's resentments.

I was not privy to the living room and boardroom arguments among family members; however, Harry and Frank were, and they reported screaming matches. Owen was a mild sort of man who was not emotionally equipped to sustain a fight, especially one against his sisters. He was deeply hurt that they had turned against him. A seemingly happy family had been disrupted, perhaps because of unseen, long-standing troubles. As soon as Owen assumed the presidency, he began to lose sleep and was overcome by anxiety. Before long, his doctor sent him to the Bahamas for a rest. Taking advantage of Owen's absence, Ed Davis tried to dominate the board and raised hard questions about coverage and circulation with the publisher and the editor. Owen returned to find a greater mess and resolved that drastic action was necessary. He decided to sell the paper.

He intended to rely on Adams and Smith to find a buyer that would keep standards high. But as soon as the word was out that the paper was on the market, a number of buyers appeared, and the issue became one of purchase price rather than the paper's character. The only competitors were large holding companies, each of which ran numerous papers as businesses. Harry and Frank knew what that meant for them and the paper. The newspaper would become a business for making money, and profit would be the chief criterion for success. The managers of the holding companies were businessmen, not journalists.

Owen did not want this at all. He regarded himself as the custodian of years of service to the community; however, he could not stand the conflicts any longer. He decided to sell to a combination of papers all over the country that were owned by a large middle-western paper. Everyone was paid off, but family relations still did not improve. It was not the money that split the family in so many ways but the various problems of the family itself, and no one could have prevented that eruption.

Molly and I wondered what would happen to me. The parent paper announced that Harry and Frank would keep their jobs. We rode along that way for a year or so. We received a pamphlet guide to newspaper management suggesting ways to maximize profit, but it was not clear that we needed to do much more, because the paper was profitable. Nevertheless, pressure for profits was relentless in the form of memos from headquarters. When we were asked to eliminate the one-person Washington bureau, we were cut off from some coverage of North Carolina affairs in Washington, and we lost the one avenue of advancement for talent recruited by the paper. We were told to print more entertaining stories, focusing on human interest, Hollywood, and sports. Local business leaders who had been intimidated by the Ravenal family and its bank began to lobby the new board, which consisted of people like themselves, about stories they did not like. Harry tried to stop this but was overruled. The paper had been traditionally Democratic, but two leading conservative columnists were added to the op-ed page. It became harder to attract smart young aspirants to the paper. We were no longer a beacon of any kind.

Harry and Frank fought all these changes while they tried to keep the peace. It did not work. I arrived at work one day only to be told that both had been fired and that new men were taking their jobs. Imagine the shock not only to me but also to the entire paper and much of the city. The new publisher and editor came from the parent paper and arrived within a few days. I knew the editor, Karl Evans, who had edited several papers in the chain. He was a utility manager to shape up acquisitions. The new publisher was Paul Engle, a business and advertising specialist from headquarters. Business was their only interest.

I met with them individually and then together. They told me that I was doing a good job but that we needed to increase profitability by cutting costs and shifting the focus of stories. The paper was a business for them regardless of the product, which could have been plumbing fixtures for all they cared. They had no sense that they might have been destroying a valuable property that had earned money year in and year out. They wanted increased profits in the short term.

I told them that I would stay for year or two if we could keep our journalistic standards high. They agreed, but they didn't mean it. They replaced editing and reportorial staff with people from their other papers in a process that could only be called "dumbing down." The quality of reporting and writing suffered, and it became apparent that they held on to me only because I had a good reputation in the business.

After Molly and I discussed our options—and we didn't talk too long—I walked into Evans's office and resigned. He didn't seem sorry, and I was soon replaced by a veteran hack from the parent paper. I had to refigure what I thought would be the last episode of my working life. We moved back to our old house in Baltimore, which had been rented all these years, and began a new life in 1996.

CHAPTER 11

Wives
Their Retrospectives

Sally (John's First Wife)

I had never met anyone like John. The boys at home were tied into local careers and their families and were very comfortable, but there wasn't much challenge. Most of my friends wanted lives like their mothers had, and even though I loved my mother, I wanted something different. I found it and loved it for a time, especially with John. But I could not sustain a new life for reasons that I still do not fully understand. I had an early romance with New York City, and John was part of that romance. He was also a southerner, and my parents liked him. He seemed to offer an exciting life.

Our first years of marriage were wonderful. We had three happy children, earned plenty of money, and lived quite well, enjoying the city, travel, and vacations. I found plenty of part-time work as an assistant to art curators, a docent, and a board member of museums. We kept close ties to Richmond and Gibson Island. I went along with John on medical trips all over the world. We had friends in the country and abroad, but psychiatrists were not really my cup of tea. Many of them in those years were Jewish, and I felt slight differences that I could not articulate. My own friends in New York were married to lawyers and businessmen, whereas, aside from psychiatrists, John's friends were writers and professors. Our dinner parties didn't work if we mixed our friends, so they were all one or the other. We noticed the discordance but didn't talk about it. His friends were Democrats, and mine were Republicans, which didn't matter during the Eisenhower years but fostered tensions later.

John traveled a lot on his own, giving talks and leading seminars. It was part of his growing professional reputation, which he valued highly. That happened with academic people. They became captured by their reputation and had to polish it for fear of losing it. We often talked with George about it, but he seemed to care much less about it than John did. George was happy to write good books that were well received. He did not want to be a "star." John did want stardom, perhaps in part because he saw himself as an original thinker and innovator in psychiatry. He was also more driven than George was.

He was always good with the children when he was in town, going to plays and sporting events, suggesting books for them to read, and he read to them at night during their dinner if he was home. But I felt that I was being pushed into the background. If I complained, he took me out to dinner for a nice evening, but those times together were sparse.

We went home to see his parents fairly often, and they were nice but uninteresting people. I couldn't help comparing the town to Richmond, which was not fair, but it seemed awfully provincial. By the same token, John was never too happy on Gibson Island. He had little in common with the comfortable, prosperous, and certainly self-satisfied business and professional men there, and their wives were even less appealing to him as conversation partners. He found the occasional individual, usually a doctor with whom he could talk, and he and my father liked each other and enjoyed going fishing together. The children were always fun for him, and they adored him. But he was bored after two weeks, and the children and I often stayed for a month or so after he left.

In the summer of 1975, the children and I stayed, and I spent some time with Charlie Best, whom I had dated in college. He was now a lawyer in Richmond. I had gone to New York after school, and he had married a lovely girl from home who had died of cancer. Charlie was now raising their two daughters with the help of his mother. We had not seen much of each other but were brought together at a cocktail party, and he charmed me all over again. He reminded me of home and of all the good things I missed. Charlie took the children sailing a few times, something that John could not do because he was not a sailor, and they immediately loved it and began lessons. We met his daughters, and our girls got along well with them. My parents were friends of his parents, and they liked Charlie, too. They didn't seem to notice that I was spending time with him, although Mother later told me that she had been concerned about me.

On a hot, mid-August day, Charlie and I played tennis, but the game was really a play of sexual energy. We touched each other every time we exchanged courts. Something was going on that neither of us wanted to stop. After the game, I invited him back to our house for a drink, and the inevitable kiss and embrace took place. We didn't say much after that, and he went home; however, my life had changed. We talked a few times after that about our lives. He was lonely, and he pulled my dissatisfactions about life in Manhattan out of me. I told him that I loved John but that he was so absorbed in his work that he had little time for me. As I think about it now, many years later, I suspect that John was growing in his understanding of himself and of human personality in ways that I could not enter, even if I had been invited. Exploration of the human soul was a lonely business.

Charlie listened but did not say much, only advising me to return to New York and work through my doubts about the marriage for myself. He said that he loved me but did not want to break up my marriage. I agreed, and the children and I went home in time for school. I settled into my usual routines but kept thinking of Charlie despite myself.

John sensed that something was wrong. He could see that I was distracted and listless. Of course, the whole story came out. One had to tell the truth to a person like John, and he could listen to the truth. Perhaps he should have fought harder to keep me, but the detachment he brought to patients may have protected him from being hurt. Or perhaps it was his respect for my distress, which he would have had for a patient. I felt terrible about what was happening, because John had been so good to me. He had encouraged me to live my own life just as he lived his, but neither of us realized that we had grown apart for that very reason. The bond was broken permanently. He must have acknowledged it as he let me go.

To explain the return to Richmond to the children, I deceived them by saying that their father would follow. It was not even a trial separation. He was not leaving his work, and I was tired of the tribes of New York and wanted to return to my own tribe. My parents were worried because they liked John, but they loved having me home, too. As Charlie became part of my life, they relaxed and accepted the reality. The children did not like Richmond at first, particularly young John, who was a New Yorker, but the girls soon adapted. John missed his father and often talked to him on the telephone. Fortunately, he was off to Yale and his father in 1980. He was always good to me, but he was his father's son in every way.

My marriage to John had been an adventure with much happiness, yet it had failed. My life in New York had been like a pleasant dream, but I had woken up and returned to an old dream.

Peggy (George's Wife)

My childhood on the Philadelphia mainline was secure and uneventful, but I always wanted out. My father was a stockbroker, and my mother was a volunteer who was too intelligent for the life she led. I was smart, too, and went to Radcliffe when my friends were going to Smith and Vassar. I knew that I wanted to be a star, a somebody, to make a difference and be noticed. I studied Romantic poetry because the poets evoked my wish and need to express my feelings. Graduate school studies could kill feelings, but I gravitated to the new criticism, which explored meanings and feelings from the language itself.

Teaching at Brown was an opportunity to help students find their own feelings through poetry. I taught and wrote about Wordsworth, Keats, Shelly, and Byron and eventually went on to Swinburne and other pre-Raphaelites.

When I met him, George struck me as a romantic because of his passion for the New Deal and its forerunners. He anchored some of his ideas in Walt Whitman, Mark Twain, and the dramas of reform in American politics. Only later did he formulate a "realism" that was more skeptical of reform. He did not like the seemingly utopian ideas of the sixties and returned to skepticism about power consistent with his own southern biases, although he was certainly a progressive. I could never fathom that blend of conservative and progressive, and he himself often had trouble with it.

His father was a nice man, and I liked his mother at first because she was a strong romantic character who almost seemed to step out of an antebellum parlor. Her act did not wear well over time, because she was acting out who she thought she was or should be and the real person was long buried; she was just a collection of mannerisms then. George loved to go home to see his parents and friends. I tolerated it for a while but did not find any of them interesting.

As we moved into the sixties, the students changed. They improved academically every year and grew more restless. The Vietnam War changed it all, especially as faculty members and students joined together in opposition of the war. Campus issues like parietal rules, coed housing, and curricular reform were infused with extra energy. I remember a university chaplain telling me that we "had to follow the kids," as if they were prophets, and indeed to many of us, they were. Moderates like George straddled fences, and that was true of most historians, political scientists, and economists. The leading radicals among the faculty came from the physics and English departments.

I got caught up into it all, particularly with the women's movement, and acted as an advocate for women's studies in the curriculum as separate programs, along with black studies and other multicultural ventures. We began to insist on more faculty appointments for women, and in a stroke of luck, Brown was put under a federal court order to hire more women after one department recommended a woman for tenure and then told the provost they did not really want her. I was being politicized because I had become romantic about social and political causes. I enjoyed participating in antiwar marches and speaking for reform within the university. My interest in the new criticism of the Romantic poets diminished, and I moved to what was to be called "cultural studies" in which culture was to be understood according to hidden power and prejudice against free expression and opportunity, especially against women and minorities. My book on women authors in modern literature was well received during that time.

George believed that women's and minority studies should have been taught within departments and disciplines, and he distrusted fashionable ideologies that seemed to be shallow ways to win advancement for young scholars. Slogans of "revolution" appalled him. He thought in terms of New Deal and Great Society concrete achievements. Politics should not promise more than it could achieve. He was not a conservative, and he did not approve of the war; however, he saw it as the consequence of Cold War politics that had overreached reality in order to resist communism. He was always confident that political reality would emerge to correct past blunders. I was not so hopeful, because I had implicitly taken on a romantic Marxist edge, without being a Marxist, believing that the American government was in the grip of forces that would prevent reform. This was all a little vague in my mind then, but in retrospect, I know that my feelings were authentic.

George and I decided to separate and then divorce without a lot of fuss. We had no children to hold us together. We had virtually ceased to be friends. George was sad, because he had wanted to be happily married. He was made for marriage. Being married was less important to me, and I was relieved when he left for the University of Virginia.

Molly (Clay's Wife)

I had a very happy childhood. My father was a museum curator in Baltimore, and my mother was a portrait painter. I went to public school and then to Bryn Mawr, where I studied art and history. After graduation, I began work at the Maryland Historical Society, writing for and eventually editing the society's magazine. I wrote about Maryland history and art and became a consultant to museums and historical renewal projects. I lived with other girls for a time until they leaped into marriage.

There were no interesting boys for me until I met Clay when friends set us up. He was different from any man I had ever met, because he reached out to people from his own happiness. He could enjoy them because he enjoyed himself. He was curious about everyone and everything, which was the journalist in him. Our enthusiasm for life was strongest when we were together. We knew right away that we were going to marry.

I did not like his working nights. The *Sun* was a whole way of life that captured its members in a crazy fellowship of camaraderie and kept them out late. He gave one night a week to our daughter when he was off. I enjoyed him the other nights and in the daytime until he went to work. Fortunately, I could work at home much of the time. His schedule was better in London and Washington, and my life was enhanced through the interesting people that we both met in our work.

John and George were such good friends. They took me in as one of them, because they were initially bachelors in Baltimore, and Clay and I looked after them. I got to know Sally and Peggy pretty well, although there wasn't any closeness among the three of us. One could easily see that the marriages were growing shaky. Clay and I listened to John and George's confessions. They understood the mistakes they had made, but neither had a clear idea about what a good marriage constituted. I finally decided that they would have to be captured by women who understood and wanted them and could teach them how to be married.

Clay loved being a managing editor, and the sale of the paper was a huge disappointment to him. He was excited about a new career, and then we had to start all over again. We found a way by becoming professional partners in writing, each stimulating the work of the other. He wrote for the *New Yorker* and the New York *Review of Books*, usually on economic policy and politics. I wrote on historical questions: What was the real relationship between Thomas Jefferson and Sally Hemmings? It was a happy life, and we had plenty of time to see our friends all over the map.

Our daughter practiced family law in Baltimore and had three children. My prediction came true about George and John after they met Julie and Anne. They captured and made their men happy, and we love them for it now. The men still love to go home to the lake and remember themselves as boys, and we women play along.

Julie (John's Second Wife)

I was born in 1940 in St. Louis to a family of comfortable means. My parents and their friends were conventional in their values and beliefs. I went to Vassar, as my mother had done, and I married a Princeton boy who took me to Chicago so that he could practice law. After five years and no children, I went to Northwestern to study clinical psychology simply because it interested me. I was beginning to outgrow my origins. My life then collapsed and was gradually transformed after my husband was killed in an airplane crash. I was a thirty-five-year-old widow with a new diploma and no plans. I thought about moving back to St. Louis but feared that family would smother me, so I stayed and worked into the practice of clinical psychology. The work was enjoyable, but I was lonely. None of the men I met, especially the psychiatrists, interested me. When I met John in 1985, I could see that he was special, because he was an explorer, and so was I in a more modest way. We were curious about human nature beyond the confines of our profession. John was such a good psychiatrist, especially as a diagnostician, that he was respected by his colleagues despite his various adventures.

I had worked with both children and adults and engaged in art and music therapy, and all of this was interesting to him. But our connection was more than intellectual; it was passionate and sensual. We knew it within a few minutes of meeting. We simply could not stay away from each other. Young John and I also fell into a kind of platonic love. He wanted me as his father's wife and his friend, a role his mother had not fully played. The two girls in Richmond loved their father and were welcoming to me. I eventually met Sally and Charlie, and there was a general feeling all round that things had turned out well.

John realized that he had neglected Sally from an obsession with his work. I could soften his drives by participation in that work. He had been driven all his life by the need to prove something. Perhaps it was the loss of his mother who was not there to stand behind him as he fought his demons. I helped relax this compulsion by giving him the emotional security that he needed.

Anne (George's Second Wife)

I was blessed to be born and raised in Annapolis amid the meadows and the sea. My parents made sailboats, and my world was the outdoors. I missed the ocean while I was a student at Duke, where I studied theater in hopes of becoming an actress. My career with auditions in New York was brief because my own intuitions and the kindness of others told me that I was not good enough.

One of my professors suggested that I teach drama, so I eventually received a doctorate from NYU and landed my first job at UVA. I taught drama and directed plays there. What could have been more fun than to teach and practice what you loved? I married a department colleague, and we lived and worked happily together for a few years; however, he liked the girls. We had no children, so he adopted his students, finally taking one of them to California with him. I decided that he was an overage flower child.

At first, I felt an inner ache, but I loved my work. George had also been hurt, and we filled our mutual emptiness with each other. He wasn't easy to live with, because he could be moody and sometimes overcritical of everyone, including himself. He was a political liberal and cultural conservative who was unhappy with modern America.He had hope for politics but very little hope for the quality of our society. He may have been an elitist without realizing it, not liking popular society yet still hoping for leadership from the top.

I got to know John, Clay, Julie, and Molly, and I liked all of them. We traveled to see each other often and sometimes took vacations together. The wives enjoyed the closeness of the three husbands because it bound us all together. I did not know Peggy, of course, but was curious about her and happened to meet her at an annual meeting of the Modern Languages Association. I heard her read a paper that made no sense to me and introduced myself to her later. She pretended that she had not known that George had remarried and was not at all friendly, so I cut the conversation off. She had not remarried, according to George. Perhaps she was still carrying a grudge. Who knew, and who cared?

We have a good life together now. I am writing a book on Shakespeare's comedies, and George is writing about senators in history. He has plunged back into teaching undergraduates with great enthusiasm, his first love, and wins prizes for teaching on occasion. We expect to slide into formal retirement without any great change in our lives. We miss not having had children, but one might say that the students have been our children.

CHAPTER 12

Homecoming

The three friends had settled down by the turn of the twenty-first century.

John and Julie had turned their projects over to others and were primarily working with patients and writing about human lives for a general but educated audience. They divided their time between New York and a beach house on the outer banks of North Carolina. Eight grandchildren were a great joy to them. They each acted as consultants to departments of psychiatry and lectured to meetings of practioners.

George and Anne were living in Charlottesville. They had visited England a good bit so that Anne could work on Shakespeare. Anne was still directing plays, and George was teaching part-time. He assisted in a television program on Theodore Roosevelt and continued to write essays on American history. He loved teaching more than ever, from freshmen to graduate students.

Clay and Molly were fixtures in Baltimore as if they had never left. Their daughter and three grandchildren were close by. Clay continued to write for national publications about economic policy and he wrote a book about the decline of the independent press in the face of corporate mass media.

No one was thinking of retirement, because they didn't see why they couldn't continue what they were doing. They thought about death but with no great urgency. All were healthy and hoped to remain so. Few of their friends had died. They all went to church, even George in his own skeptical way, and they believed the creed they said every Sunday. Yet one would not call them devout. They were relaxed and hopeful in their faiths.

The three couples with their children and grandchildren eventually came together at the North Carolina mountain lake for July 4, 2000, and the men's seventieth birthdays. The three family houses were in good condition from years of care, and families were packed into them with overlap across houses when needed. They swam, ate hamburgers, hot dogs, and corn on the cob, and had long conversations. The three "boys," who still thought of themselves that way, bantered in conversations about their lives.It all seemed magical to them, because it was touched by friendship.

On the evening of July 4th, they ate dinner at one long table lit by candlelight. Many were enjoying chiggers, but luckily, spray kept the mosquitoes away. They ate fried chicken, ham, potato salad, corn on the cob, fresh tomatoes, ice cream, and chess pie, all washed down by beer for the grown-ups and lemonade for the striplings. Then they settled down to hear each man tell his story.

John began by saying that he had always wanted to be a healer, even before he had known what that had really meant. He thought that his mother's death might have had something to do with this impulse. He wanted to prevent pain because he had experienced a lot of pain in his childhood. Medicine seemed a good path, particularly because his father had been a doctor, and psychiatry had beckoned because it addressed psychological pain. After he practiced for some time, he discovered that curing an illness and healing meant different things in medicine, especially in psychiatry, because there were few complete cures. The best one could do most of the time was to help patients accept their illnesses through healing. They could improve their health but not make it perfect. Many had to accept limits to their psychological capacities and live with them. And yet it was possible to live happily and healed without being completely cured. In that sense, psychiatrists were doctors of souls. One taught patients to find strength to heal themselves so that body, mind, and spirit could come together.

He complimented Julie for helping to bring him to this understanding by virtue of her quiet empathy with patients. She was a godsend. He remembered his mother imperfectly, and although Julie was not a substitute mother, she had brought him an intimacy that he had perhaps lost when his mother had died. His father was a good man, and after the rift caused by the stepmother, he had established a good friendship with his father. As one aged, friends became even more important, and George and Clay had been his good friends for all of his life. Among his many friends, they were the very best.

He was amazed that he had done as well as he had in resisting the complete "medicalization" of psychiatry against strong professional and organizational imperatives. He had always thought that the effort to treat the body without concern for mind and spirit would fall short. He felt that perhaps the tide was turning. It was an argument for sticking to your guns.

He had great hope for his three children and eight grandchildren, all of whom were present. He had been a fairly traditional person in his values and morals, and he thought that they were much the same. But they were walking on altogether new paths. His son, the actor, was teaching theater. One of his daughters had become an Episcopal priest in her thirties and was serving an inner-city parish in Richmond. The other daughter was running a business with her husband. He could see his parents in their faces—the biological ties that bound them together.

George said that he was a teacher, whether in the classroom or at his desk writing books. In the broadest sense, he was teaching about the American experiment. America had been founded on ideals, and the dynamic to remember, recreate, and realize them would persist. Competing ideals were expressed in politics, which was good, and no one ever won completely. He was a progressive but not a utopian, and he had fought on two fronts against standpatters and radicals, because each extreme denied James Madison's understanding of human nature, which suggested that we were not perfectly virtuous but able to guard against our worst motives through institutions that were partly designed to enhance our virtues.

He did not believe that it was easy to know what justice or any of the political virtues, such as liberty and equality, were. We discovered what these words might have meant through experience and politics. There were no philosopher kings in American democracy. George had loved universities and had been frustrated by them at the same time. They were a place to search for understanding, but often technical knowledge became an end in itself for the professional advancement of faculty members to the exclusion of broader questions. Pressures for professional and organizational prestige could contribute to disciplinary narrowness. He believed very strongly that one purpose of American history was to introduce students to the perennial questions about democracy. It was a mission with which he would charge all future historians.

He praised Anne, saying that she had saved his life by loving him and stimulating him to rediscover the excitement of studying American history and politics. He admitted that he could not have done it by himself. They had no children, but there had been compensations in generations of students.

Then he thought aloud about his parents. His father had been a superb courtroom lawyer, and he hoped that he had learned the meticulous skills of preparation and the careful judgment that his father had shown in practicing law. Perhaps it helped him become a good historian. His mother was a rare southern flower who had been born a century too late. She did not fully realize it, but she was gracious with everyone and never did a bad thing to anyone.

Clay said that he had always wanted to tell stories. He recalled Mark Twain's experience as a boy learning stories from an old black slave. Clay had been interested in human stories, and newspaper work had seemed the best way to pursue this interest. Democracy relied on stories so that people could understand themselves and their society. Newspapers, radio and television, movies, and magazines were vehicles for telling stories. Stories were one way to pull people out of passivity and thrust them into action. John and George had been students of lives; Clay hoped that he had done so as well.

Many organizations in society did not want stories to be told if the messages were contrary to their agendas. That was true of business, labor, and all kinds of organizations, perhaps government especially. Legislative politicians used rhetoric to cloud the truth, as did executives and bureaucrats, and the latter tried to quiet or distort stories. The disappointment of his life emerged when news-gathering organizations distorted, biased, or held back stories for profit. Reporting had lost its autonomy, and we were all poorer for it.

Clay could not say enough about Molly. She was calm, strong, and happy, and he could not sink too deeply into the dumps without her pulling him out and dusting him off. "Marriage was of equals," he said, "but men may need women especially because men are so unsteady in their natures." This view might not have been politically correct, but he believed it anyway. He knew he and the others valued their wives not just as companions and lovers but as persons in their own right, and yet they were traditional men of their generation who believed that they could not have achieved what they had done without the love of their wives. And it was true.

Clay admired his father, the banker, who worked very hard to use the bank to help families throughout their region. His father had seen the bank as an agent for change rather than a moneymaker, and he was happy that his first cousin, John Page, was doing his best to keep up the tradition. Then he remembered his mother. He had read her journals and was now working to get her poems published. The journals had been very private to her and not meant for anyone to read, but she had not destroyed them.

His daughter now had them and would keep them for her children and grandchildren. They drew a picture of a woman who had accepted life as it was given to her and who could yet see the rare colors of beauty and tenderness that had given her peace. She would continue to speak to her descendants in the far future.

These men were their parents' children in the sense that their parents had created a solid foundation for their growth. None of the boys was closed off from the possibility of growth. The three boys had had more opportunities and more scope to be creative. Yet they were still southerners in many ways. Mark Twain had once said that you could take the boy out of Missouri but could never take Missouri out of the boy. They had blended their past with their lives in recognizable ways. They could not explain their ambition to do well, although they could see the course this impulse had taken in their own lives. Perhaps Dr. Bob McIver, DD, had influenced them to find their vocations after all.

All of us are on a journey to become full versions of our better selves. This was what was interesting about the lives of these men. They could not tell the future, but their lives had made them hopeful. What more could one ask?

AFTERWORD

My friend Dr. Alex McLeod was a great help with medical and stylistic matters. Dimples Kellogg was a marvelous editor. Jack May, Jacque Voegeli, and Frank Somerville read the novel and made helpful suggestions. Juanita Cate suggested that the subjects write their chapters in the first person. I feel comfortable with university and newspaper life and have some understanding of psychotherapy and psychiatry, but I also relied on the following books about medical education: Howard S. Becker's *Boys in White* (1961), Melvin Kumar, *Becoming a Doctor* , Clifton K. Meador's *Med School: A Collection of Stories about Medical School, 1951–1955* (2003), and David Viscott's *The Making of a Psychiatrist* (1972). James D. Squires's *Read All About It: The Corporate Takeover of America's Newspapers* (1993) gave historical context, and R. H. Gardner's *Those Years: Recollections of a Baltimore Newspaperman* (1990) is a wonderful view of life on the *Sun*.

ABOUT THE AUTHOR

Erwin Hargrove is a professor emeritus of political science at Vanderbilt University. His bachelor's and doctoral degrees are from Yale. He taught at Brown University from 1960 to 1976 and Vanderbilt from 1976 to 2000. His academic specialty has been presidential leadership. He and his wife Julie live in Nashville.

Manufactured By: RR Donnelley
                     Breinigsville, PA USA
                     February, 2011